SAME
BED,
DIFFERENT
DREAMS

HUGH GROSS

3/5/93

MID-LIST PRESS
Denver   Minneapolis

F I R S T   N O V E L   S E R I E S

Published by Mid-List Press, P.O. Box 200292, Denver, CO 80220

Library of Congress Cataloging-in-Publication Data

Gross, Hugh, 1955-
   Same bed, different dreams / Hugh Gross
      p.   cm.
      ISBN 0922811-10-5: $17.95—ISBN 0-922811-11-3 (pbk): $9.95
      I. Title
   PS3557.R575S35   1991
   813' .54--dc20   91-9684
                                         CIP

Manufactured in the USA

ACKNOWLEDGEMENTS

I would like to thank my parents Earl and Mindy—for everything—and my brother David too.

I would also like to express my appreciation to Jolene Lee, Barbara Dalton-Taylor, Linda Hitomi Saito, Kaori Minami and her family, Alan Patterson, Kyoko Yamauchi, Masao Yamauchi, Brooke Jacobson, Kazuko Hashimoto, Naomi Matsumoto, Genshi Shigekawa, Johnny Amato, Barry Gooley, Reiko Bradley, Matt Bearson, Carl Bressler, Kenny Tasaka, Asako Torigoe, Sugao Kawamura, Ronald Springwater, Jacqueline Springwater, Richard Gunther, Mark Taylor, Sam Chauncey, Ronald Hartwick, Joseph Kleinman, Dennis Friedman, Robert Rotwein, Cathy Martino, Robert Sharp, Robert Maurer, James Thornton, Adam Blumenstein, Robert Goldfarb, and the Fukumi and Edleson families.

Finally, I wish to thank all my Japanese and American teachers, hosts, friends and students, whom I have been unable to name here, for their spirit and generosity.

ONE

Toshio took the train. A commute he had made every weekday morning, on one route or another, from the age of six. First to school, now to work. Being president of his own company, he could have driven or arranged to be chauffeured. The chief was entitled. Crowded as it was, however, the train had become too much a part of his routine to give up. Too fixed a part of what pressed him into the day. The best time for thinking, the best time for working things out.

Toshio habitually studied the other passengers. This morning as the train pulled out he noticed a few familiar faces, but no one he really knew. Certainly no one to speak with. That was fine. Toshio did not look for old friends on the train. He looked for pretty girls.

Around him some people were reading. A few closed their eyes. The majority were standing, trying to steady themselves with one hand while talking, or reading what they could hold with their free hand, or doing nothing.

Another activity took place on crowded trains, buses and subways—an activity in which not everyone took part and in which others, had the choice been their own, would assuredly have preferred not to participate. To put it simply, some men took advantage of the overcrowded conditions to press up against or use their hands on women who were standing next to them. The rules were straightforward. The activity should not be seen. Regardless of the developing situation one's face should reflect little more than indifference toward another selfsame day. Under no circumstances should there be any acknowledgement of the woman.

The situation was not easily faced by offended women. Attributing intention was rude. There were times for men, as well, when through no one's fault, a potentially embarrassing physical position was created through lack of space. The most distressing moments could actually involve an acquaintance. With a stranger at least it was possible to position one's arms or turn away, to push off or ask what the other person was doing.

Toshio understood the frustration of the train. The effort to steal something for oneself between the endless obligations: school, job, family, country. The difference between the world of heroic exploits, of romantic encounters pictured in the popular cartoon books written for adults and widely read on the train, and the day-to-day reality, which always seemed to say there was something else to do. Perhaps with the group. To help.

And of his own experience. Oh, to have been born twenty, thirty years later! The freedom, the tolerance. The opportunities. Toshio had always been required to be somewhere, to be busy with something, to be accounted for. An inseparable part of the whole, with anything left over largely a matter of chance. Toshio could not remember when growing up having ever been left alone with a girl his own age. For that matter, he could not remember a feeling of having ever been left alone at all.

And so in his youth he learned to compensate by going where others could not find him. To imaginary accomplishments, conversations, meetings, girlfriends, meetings, accomplishments, sex. While riding trains, while running errands, while sitting in class.

Toshio had particularly liked the anonymity and crush of the train. And as a young man, in his general discouragement and perhaps against his better nature, he had allowed himself to transgress. To throw out a hand, little more than a floppy fish, hoping that the press of the crowd would take it where he could not put it himself. Where it should not be. To be sure, many times he directed himself with thoughts of school, success, career, country, castigating himself for lack of discipline. Temporarily. He could not distract himself from his growing preoccupation.

He knew he was not alone. Adult magazines and the even more explicit comic books were commonly read on the train. When someone left a copy behind, Toshio picked it up. Making jokes for consolation, to ease his tension. People think about sex and their work, he told himself.

Toshio thought hard in those days about who was having sex. He wasn't. Somewhere not so far away, Toshio knew, there were prostitutes. And a rich man could have a mistress. But what use was this to him? Prostitutes were for men who worked. He had no money at that time. If the world of chance encounters and secret trysts pictured in the magazines and comic books existed, Toshio could not find it. The truth—he became convinced to his disappointment—was that most sex actually took place between married couples. The rest seemed to involve a small group of sexually active women who were as yet unavailable to him: a few women who seemed to be having sex with an awful lot of men. Although Toshio was not pleased with the immediate implications of his conclusions, he could not convince himself he was wrong.

Sex had not been isolated as bad, wrong or unnatural. But the interactions that might lead to sex had been eliminated.

Toshio now thought about his wife Nozomi. The way she moved, her tone of voice, the way she asked him what he wanted, the way she smelled. Her tone of life. How lately everything about her . . .

Nozomi, he said to himself, all day long I answer questions. I sit at a desk, I talk on the phone. At home I don't want to answer questions, I don't want to discuss the day. I don't want to think about the office. I answer questions all day. Do I have to do that now?

The train moved forward. Toshio noticed a few familiar faces, but no one he really knew. That was fine. Toshio did not look for old friends on the train. He continually looked for pretty girls so that if circumstances allowed, if he was standing next to one and could face her, if he was sure that he would not be seen, then he could allow the weight of the crowd to push him in. Gradually. From behind. From the side. Straight on. So that she felt him. Unmistakably. Usually the woman reacted, pushed him away, or positioned a book, an arm, a bag. But sometimes she chose to take it, to stand passively instead. Toshio did not know why. But he did know that if he met her eyes he would always see anger as well as shame.

The train unloaded at Shinjuku. Toshio's stop was a large, modern station surrounded by skyscrapers on one side and by shorter six-to-ten-story buildings on the other. On the way to his office Toshio walked past an off-track betting shop, past *pachinko* pinball parlors, past magazine stands, past discount electronics stores. Some days Toshio would pick out an attractive woman and follow her, perhaps only for a block or two. Not even to make contact. Every

4

morning he procrastinated, resisting the force that inevitably pulled him to his desk.

Toshio did not work for any of the large corporate groups. He did not work for the national telephone monopoly, nor for the national television station. Neither did he work for the national bureaucracy, as did his brother Kazuo. He did not work in high technology, capital equipment, international trade or finance. He ran a small advertising company. Which is to say he now had money, but that real status in his society had eluded him. He sometimes told himself that men were the same wherever. A little bit of ashtray in everyone, he mused, but he wished he had been more sure.

His brother Kazuo, by comparison, did not make as much money, but did hold a more secure position. Kazuo, who studied hard and passed his entrance examinations, had entered a good public university, then landed the right job. A position Toshio detested, precisely because it was a job with the government, the foreign service. "He hasn't even been to Hokkaido," Toshio liked to say.

From the time they were children Kazuo had always done the right thing before their parents. Toshio never had. For Toshio, schoolwork was uninteresting, ceremony boring, manners overdrawn. Toshio had been caught in the wrong place and time. Smart was not enough. Position required other characteristics as well. Patience. Grace. Connections. But at least business suited him better than school had. Business was easy, he thought. It had to be.

Toshio's success was such that he managed to buy a home for his parents as well as for his own family. And while he expected his mother to respond more favorably to his gesture than she had, there were several continuing consolations. One: other than temporary situations such as the fiasco that occurred when Toshio had to replace their plumbing, his parents were essentially precluded from moving in with Nozomi and himself. While his parents had lived with Kazuo's family in the cramped apartment and Toshio's family had been in their more comfortable, larger, new house, there had existed a definite tension. Buying the second home was an insurance policy on the benefits of the first. Two: Toshio did not pretend to be a model husband, but buying the house for his parents had allowed him to come as close as he could toward achieving certain fundamentals. There was a saying that listed the qualities a desirable husband should have: "House, car, no mother-in-law." Toshio had done his best. Three: as irksome as his mother's continuing complaints could be, at least she did keep the issue well-placed as an irritant before Kazuo who had refused out of pride to move his family into the home that Toshio had bought. It was one of the few clear victories Toshio had been able to gain at his brother's expense. After a lifetime of feeling second-best, it was worth whatever the cost. Toshio saw too much weakness in his brother to respect him or his job. Where they tell you what kind of tie to put on in the morning. How to entertain guests. Toshio did not like his brother's wife either. And his children were annoying.

"Looks like I missed the company song," Toshio said to his receptionist, who stood and bowed to greet him when he arrived in his office at ten after nine. Many corporations began each working day with a few calisthenics and a company song. In fact, Toshio's company, Diamond Advertising, did not. "I run an unusual agency," he told clients on occasion when they were drinking. "The only office in Japan where everyone leaves at five."

The Diamond Advertising Company occupied one floor of a small office building. There was a reception area, a conference room, a computer room, a kitchen used mainly

6

for making coffee and tea, Toshio's private office, and a general bull pen area for the fourteen "salarymen,"who will work until retirement at fifty-five, and the ten to twelve "office ladies"—young women who come into an office at twenty-one or twenty-two and who leave when they get married at about twenty-three or twenty-four. As Toshio walked through the bull pen this morning he felt an unusual buzz. He assumed they were talking about him.

"Chuo line," he said and forced a smile. His commuter train.

Toshio's secretary, Mitsue, handed Toshio his phone messages. In spite of the enthusiasm Mitsue had brought to the firm when she began eighteen months before, Toshio had seen her work become less consistent.

"Tea?" she asked.

Toshio shook his head no.

"Coffee?"

"No, thanks," he said, "already nervous."

She smiled. Toshio had hired the most unattractive secretary he could find. He had learned the hard way about the other kind.

Out of the corner of his eye he noticed one of his younger salarymen approaching him. Toshio was not ready to begin the day. "Close the door behind you," he told Mitsue, a signal he did not wish to be disturbed.

Toshio looked at his desk. Too much mail, too many messages. Resisting any rational inclination to organize himself, he cleared a space and opened the morning's business daily, the *Japan Economic Journal.* The national weather satellite had failed. Maybe that will improve the forecast, he thought. The stock market had been down. Why does that make me happy?

He routinely checked the prices of stocks he had already sold, often seeing that he had closed out a position too soon.

Stocks, he discovered, moved too slowly to suit his temperament. He still traded occasionally, but found commodities to be more interesting. Toshio traded *azuki* beans, a small red bean that had been nicknamed "The Red Diamond," because so much money had been made and lost on it so quickly. Toshio kept his own chart on the daily price movement of the *azuki* bean contract. A slow day in the office meant at least two calls to his broker. Toshio liked trading commodities. If not for the commissions, he thought, he might even have made money.

Mitsue came on the intercom. "Mr. Ozaki on line three," she said. Shun Ozaki was possibly Toshio's most important business relationship. There was no question that she should put this call through.

Shun Ozaki had begun thirty-two years before with a single lease on a small sushi location in downtown Tokyo. His innovation had been to introduce a conveyor belt that carried little trays of the raw fish around the counter like baggage goes round at the airport. Although it was clever at the time, many others soon copied it. In fact, Shun Ozaki never made much money with sushi. The first real money he made was by passing along his lease.

Ozaki took advantage of two system quirks to amass his fortune. The first was that developers of new buildings were often so anxious while construction was under way that they would make extremely favorable arrangements with a desirable first tenant knowing that later it would be easier to rent to others if some space was already filled. Ozaki moved quickly to be a first tenant whenever possible, negotiating long-term leases with advantageous terms. Real estate values, rents and leases had been a one-way street in Tokyo. Up. The key to what Ozaki later received in selling his franchise locations was almost always the underlying lease he buried in the deal.

There was another aspect to his operation, more important recently. In opening his sushi shops, later laundromats and grocery stores, Ozaki found that he could borrow money at reasonably modest interest rates. During his business career he had generally paid under ten percent. Others without a business of their own or without collateral paid finance companies at the astonishing rate of forty percent to as much as seventy-two percent. Ozaki's most profitable current operation was borrowing at less than ten percent and lending at more than forty percent. Stories about salarymen killing themselves and their families because a loan collector had run through their neighborhood shouting that they had failed to meet a financial obligation were common knowledge. Shun took a softer approach. Choose your borrowers carefully and collection would not be a problem. The other operations, the front of his empire: sushi chain, gas stations, dry cleaners, et cetera, served as the break-even window dressing that allowed him to borrow more and more money for his lending activities. Toshio's job was to highlight the window dressing, most recently the sushi chain.

"But what kind of fool borrows at interest rates like those?" Nozomi had asked.

"You'd be surprised," Toshio answered.

None other than Shun Ozaki had financed Toshio's acquisition of Diamond Advertising. As a salaryman in the company himself, Toshio had no other means of raising money when the former owner had suddenly passed away. Given the short-term nature of the opportunity, the nervousness of the estate, and his inability to raise funds from other quarters, Toshio had considered the interest rate to be irrelevant and would have gladly paid higher.

The other occasion on which Toshio had borrowed was more embarrassing. Illiquid and caught short against four horrendous days holding too many *azuki* bean contracts was not an experience he wanted to repeat. Having delayed too long, Toshio placed himself in a same-day need situation, desperate and with serious possible consequences. "It happens to the best of us," Ozaki had said on the phone. The cash was delivered immediately, about as much money again as Toshio had borrowed only four years earlier to finance his purchase of Diamond Advertising.

"Shun Ozaki on line three," Mitsue repeated.

"I'll take it," Toshio said.

"Moshi, moshi," he heard.

"Moshi, moshi," Toshio answered. "Mr. Ozaki, how are you? It's been too long."

"Evidently," Ozaki said. "I'm surprised you took the call."

Toshio paused. He could never understand Ozaki's sense of humor. "Well," Toshio said, "I didn't see how it could be you this early in the morning."

Ozaki laughed hard. Coughed and laughed again, "Oh, Matsuzaka," he always called Toshio by his last name, "forgive me for dispensing with the small talk."

"Of course," Toshio said. "What can I do for you?"

"I have a letter on my desk," Ozaki continued, "concerning the Big Catch ads." Big Catch was the name of Ozaki's sushi chain.

Toshio wondered which of his salarymen had screwed up this time. Zen mind, he counseled himself.

"From a committee of the national PTA," Ozaki said. "They find certain aspects of our advertising objectionable."

Toshio felt a tension in the back of his neck and a pressure around his eyes. He had pushed for this campaign. Ads that featured children dressed up and carrying on like adults in a sushi restaurant. "You're Always a Big Deal With Us." "At Big Catch Sushi You Don't Have to Be a Big Spender." The PTA objected to a cigar that one of the boys was holding and to some sake and beer that were pictured as well.

They had been together too long—so Toshio did not feel in danger of losing the account. He too knew a few things about Shun Ozaki. Even bad publicity was not always bad, he reminded himself. As long as people thought that Ozaki's business was business, that was the important thing. After all, Toshio's job had been to create a bigger presence in the community.

But then not exactly this kind of presence either, he thought. The activity level was an entirely different question. They would certainly abandon this campaign, money that would not easily flow again soon. Toshio did not like to cancel what was already on line. But besides the money involved, besides the inconvenience and the loss of goodwill, it irritated Toshio to be at any further disadvantage to Shun Ozaki than already necessary. He thought about whom he could blame.

The phone disconnected.

"Your wife on line three," the receptionist said over the intercom. The light was blinking.

Furious, Toshio stood up and walked out to Mitsue's desk. Another office lady was sitting there. "Where is she?" Toshio asked.

"She went to the bathroom," the girl replied.

"What does she do in there?" he asked. It seemed that Mitsue spent an inordinate amount of time in the bathroom.

"I don't know."

Toshio went back to his office. He took a long look at the bag of golf clubs he kept in one corner, but walked to his desk and picked up the phone. "Nozomi," he said, "unless it's an emergency . . ."

Mitsue appeared at the door. "Did you want to see me?" she asked.

"Mitsue," he said, "you go to the bathroom, I get cut off."

"Who were you speaking with?" she asked.

"Shun Ozaki."

"Do you want me to try him again?"

"Please," he said. "And send Saeki in here." Saeki was one of Toshio's most promising salarymen.

"Saeki's not here," she said. "Mr. Itoh invited him to the sumo matches."

Toshio had never considered sumo to be that interesting, but Hiroto Itoh was the agency's biggest client, sole owner of Japan's largest privately-held septic tank clean-up company. "Well," Toshio replied, "at least someone around here is doing something useful."

"Will there be anything else?" Mitsue asked.

"Just get Mr. Ozaki on the line again and tell my wife I've got calls backed up and can't talk now. And send Tahara in here, please." Tahara was the youngest salaryman in the office, having joined the spring before.

Tahara appeared at once. Despite their age difference—Tahara had just turned twenty-three—Toshio felt an inexplicable urge around him to speak openly. "Sit down," Toshio said. "Mitsue is dialing Shun Ozaki. We may have to cancel the campaign."

Tahara nodded.

Toshio did not know why he talked like this to the youngest member of his office.

"Why is this taking so long?" Toshio asked, pointing to the phone. He looked at Tahara again. "What did you do with your hair?"

12

"I had it cut."

"It looks good," Toshio said. "You'll have to show me the place." Toshio took a deep breath and put his palms over his eyes. "What else? What did they talk about yesterday?" The salarymen held a meeting each afternoon to review the office's activity. While in principle Toshio agreed these meetings were valuable, in practice he found them difficult to attend. The group tried to reach a consensus on each issue before moving to the next. There was incredible attention to detail. Then, Toshio thought, they finally get the facts right and miss the conclusion.

"We discussed the color theme for Mr. Itoh's account," Tahara said.

"I thought we had decided," Toshio said. "Pink, right?"

"There were some considerations," Tahara said. "Most of their competition uses green now."

"But that's the idea," Toshio said. "That's why we use pink."

"Ken Kondo," Mitsue said over the intercom.

"What about Ozaki?" Toshio shouted back.

"I don't think she can hear you, Chief," Tahara said.

"I know she can't hear me, Tahara," he said picking up the phone. "I know she can't hear me."

"Moshi, moshi," Kondo said.

"Moshi, moshi," Toshio said.

"Moshi, moshi," Kondo said.

"Moshi, moshi," Toshio said.

They laughed. Toshio considered Ken Kondo to be his best friend, one of a few people who could be put through directly. Their business success had come at roughly the same time, and in some sense they seemed to have grown up together. This *moshi, moshi* ritual was the remains of an inside joke, the gist of which they seemed to have forgotten, but whose punch line they persisted with anyway.

13

"How's the samurai today?" Kondo asked.

"Great," Toshio said sarcastically. "Just a second." Toshio began searching through the papers on his desk. When he found what he was looking for he came back to the phone. "Bu-e-no-su di-a-su," Toshio said. Kondo had just returned from Mexico. Being in the group travel business, he traveled frequently.

"What?" Kondo asked.

"Buenos días," Toshio repeated.

"Oh," Kondo said, *"buenos días* to you too."

Mitsue walked in and handed Toshio a note. Toshio looked at the note and momentarily lost concentration. "I can't think of anything else funny to say, Ken."

Kondo laughed anyway. "Well," he said, "I know you're busy. Specific reason for the call is this: are we still on for golf Sunday?" The two men prided themselves for having played over most of Asia.

"Unless I'm in jail," Toshio said.

Tahara laughed a little too hard at this.

"They can't do that," Kondo said. "We depend on people like you."

"For what?" Toshio asked. They laughed harder. "By the way, I want a full report on your trip to Mexico. What's it like over there?"

"It's different," Kondo said.

"A lot of Japanese cars?" Toshio asked.

"No, actually they were mostly American."

"No kidding," Toshio said. "Did you drive one?" Toshio had driven a Mercedes before, but never an American car.

"I drove a Pontiac," Kondo replied.

"And?"

"Don't worry."

14

"That's good," Toshio said. "When I see you, you'll have to give me the details. And a few things we haven't talked about . . ." Toshio winked at Tahara.

"Can do," Kondo said.

"Good," Toshio said. "Then I'll talk to you."

"Later," Kondo said. "Stop by tonight."

"Later," Toshio said.

"Later," Kondo said.

"Can you believe it?" Toshio asked Tahara. "The time I spend saying hello and good-bye with that guy." He looked again at the note Mitsue had brought in earlier. "Mitsue," he buzzed on the intercom, "what does this say?"

Mitsue came in. "What?" she asked.

"Your note," Toshio said. "What does it say?"

"Oh," she said, "Mr. Ozaki asked you to meet him at Esprit tonight around ten-thirty." Esprit was a bar that Toshio had formerly frequented. Although he would have preferred another location, under the circumstances there was no objecting.

"He didn't want to speak with me?" Toshio asked.

"He wanted to," she said, "but he said he would speak with you later."

"Mitsue," Toshio said, "if he doesn't want to speak with me now you can tell me that too."

Mitsue nodded and lowered her eyes.

"Thank you, Mitsue," he said so she could go. Toshio glanced at his appointment book. "Meeting with the American this afternoon," he said to Tahara. "You ready?"

Tahara was the office English specialist. Being the youngest, he had presumably forgotten less than the others.

"What other exciting things are going on around here that I should know about?" Toshio asked.

"Nothing really," Tahara said.

"Nothing?" Toshio feigned surprise. "Think of something."

Tahara thought. "Well," he said, "I don't know. Maybe one thing."

"Yes?"

"Didn't we ask the modeling agency to send some girls over later this afternoon for the Yamaura account?"

"That's right," Toshio said. "The cigarette lighter."

Tahara nodded.

"'Nothing,' you said! How many are coming?"

"Ten or twelve," Tahara said, "I'm not sure."

"What age group?"

"Eighteen to twenty-three."

"No kidding," Toshio said.

"No kidding."

Toshio nodded. There were worse ways to make a living. Mitsue buzzed on the intercom. "Excuse me," she said, "we have an American in the reception area. He says he has an appointment with you."

"I don't understand." Toshio looked at his appointment book, then at his watch. "I have this written down for three."

"He said he was forced to come early."

Toshio let up the intercom so Mitsue couldn't hear. "You think Mitsue got this all in English?"

Mitsue appeared at the door. "Mitsue," Toshio asked, "have you been speaking with our visitor in English?"

Mitsue sighed. "I'd like to," she said, "but he brought an interpreter."

"Really," Toshio said, "Japanese or American?"

"Japanese."

"Of course." Toshio had never had a full conversation with an American before. When he traveled, he traveled in Asia. Kondo had many opportunities because he was in the travel business, but Toshio had yet to visit North America. Many times he had thought he should. Success in Japanese advertising depended so much on one's ability to introduce the right English word or phrase.

"Well," Toshio said, "shall we meet our guest?"

"Why not?" Tahara said.

Toshio smiled. Tahara was becoming more like himself every day.

Ted Krane, the American, was about six feet tall, had sandy-brown hair and wore what Toshio might have called a business suit if it had not been beige. His appearance was a minor event at Diamond Advertising. Most of Toshio's employees had little contact with foreigners.

Krane worked for Sweet Wells, an American-based advertising company that had achieved a certain notoriety of late by losing a lawsuit filed by one of its secretaries who had been asked to type during her lunch break. More generally, Sweet Wells was known for having expanded aggressively in recent years by forming foreign affiliations. Krane's three-week trip was an overture towards a possible Sweet Wells joint venture in Japan. Krane had hired an interpreter through the Japan Travel Bureau—a young woman who had majored in English in college and then had studied for two years in England.

Toshio signaled for the four of them to move back into his office. Although he felt relieved he would not have to depend on Tahara's English skills to conduct the meeting, the presence of the interpreter inhibited Toshio. Because he was not completely sure about how to relate through her, he felt unusually hesitant. He wished her role had not been necessary. His feelings about Krane were less ambivalent. He liked him immediately. He liked his big smile and his apparent easiness. There was a freshness about Krane. He was different. Toshio also found him to be strikingly

17

handsome and imagined what an easy sex life he must have. Then Toshio experienced one of the strangest feelings he could remember. In spite of this being their first meeting and in spite of the general disinclination toward outward displays of affection, Toshio felt an urge to touch his guest. He was relieved when it passed.

Krane gave Toshio a bottle of American whiskey he had purchased earlier at the duty-free store on his flight's stopover in Hawaii. The heavy import tax made this an especially nice present and Toshio was pleased to receive it.

"*Arigato gozaimashita.*" Toshio bowed slightly to thank Krane. "Please," he said, "sit down."

"*Doomo,*" Krane replied. He liked this all-purpose word, *doomo*.

"My God, the man speaks the language," Toshio responded. "Did you study in America?"

Krane had no idea what Toshio was saying—his interpreter had taught him only a few words and expressions—so he laughed. The interpreter laughed too. Tahara laughed. Toshio laughed. No question about it. Toshio liked this guy Krane. There was a feeling of life about him.

"Tahara speaks a little English himself," Toshio told the interpreter.

"Really?" she said and translated for Krane.

"Is that right?" Krane said to Tahara in English. "How long have you been studying?"

Tahara looked at Krane, then the floor. Although he had studied English for three years in junior high school, three years in high school, one year in college and had been taking conversational English classes for the last six months at night, his experience with a native-speaker was limited, to say the least. Junior high school and high school study had focused on reading and writing skills conducted entirely in

Japanese. College study was much the same. Even the first conversational English school Tahara attended had been a disappointment. There had been almost no native-speaking teachers and the textbook they used had written the pronunciations of English words in one of the two Japanese alphabets. So Tahara changed conversational English schools, at some expense, in order to satisfy his need to study with a native-speaking teacher. But trying to figure out just what Ted Krane actually said, the only thing Tahara could think of was that he had not made this change in schools soon enough.

So much for Tahara. Toshio decided that he would conduct the interview himself through the interpreter. "How do you like Japan?" he asked Krane.

"I love it."

Toshio nodded. He knew he'd been right about this guy. "What about Japanese food?" he asked. "Do you eat sushi?"

"I like Japanese food," Krane said. "We eat sushi in New York all the time."

"Heh?" Toshio had heard about this, but he still found it hard to believe.

"You'd be surprised," Krane said. "There are sushi bars everywhere."

"And you like it?" Toshio asked.

"Sure," Krane said. "My favorite is sea urchin eggs—you know, *uni*." Krane displayed an impressive list of Japanese fish and shellfish vocabulary he had picked up at sushi bars: *maguro, ebi, hamachi, kani*.

Toshio smiled at Tahara. *"Hanbaagaa,"* he said. Hamburger.

"May I ask," Toshio continued, "how old you are?"

"I'm thirty-nine."

"Thirty-nine?" Toshio was surprised. It was hard to accept that Krane could be only three years younger than himself. "You look so young."

"How old are you?" Krane asked.

"Seventeen," Toshio said. This got a good laugh all around.

"Have you been with your company a long time?" Toshio asked.

Krane smiled sheepishly. "About eight months."

"Eight months?" Toshio asked the interpreter to make sure she had gotten this correctly. "Eight months?" he repeated. "What did you do before that?"

"I worked for another advertising company," Krane said. "Sweet Wells offered me a better opportunity."

Again Toshio had the interpreter confirm that this was exactly what Krane had said. "How did your boss react when you told him that you were leaving?"

"He wanted to know if there was a job for him too." Krane laughed.

"You hear that, Tahara?" Toshio asked.

Tahara wasn't sure what to make of this.

"Consider it this way," Krane said to Toshio, "you didn't marry the first girl you went out with, did you?"

Actually, Toshio had. The courtship lasted little more than a year.

There was an uncomfortable pause, which Toshio ended by leaning forward to look Krane directly in the eye. "What do you think of Japanese women?" he asked.

"I've only been here ten days," Krane said, "so it's hard to say."

"Of course," Toshio said.

"And I don't like to make generalizations," Krane continued, "but I like Japanese women. They seem to be very kind."

20

If you knew . . . Toshio thought. "Well," he said, "you seem to have learned a lot about Japan. But tell us your purpose. Why did you come?"

"I'd like to be straightforward," Krane said. "We think that Japan is going to become an even bigger player over the next few years. We want to be part of it."

Toshio smiled. We've only been here for two thousand years, he thought.

"Japan is an important country," Krane continued, "a dynamic country. We're hoping to develop a relationship with a company already well-placed in the market. It's been difficult for foreigners, we know. But Japan is opening up. We need each other. How long can Japan remain this isolated?"

Toshio and Tahara twisted ever so slightly, as if their ties were being tightened by the same unseen hand.

"I tried to buy an English language newspaper this morning," Krane said, "and the only ones I could find were published by Japanese companies. It was easier to find a real English newspaper when I was in Bali. Something has to change, don't you think? It doesn't make sense."

Toshio chose not to speak. Growing up, he thought, we had a saying, "When America catches cold, Japan sneezes." He took a deep breath. Ten or fifteen years from now . . . he looked at Krane . . . as China develops.

The room was quiet, the mood slightly tense. Toshio gathered his attention. He would have asked Krane about Bali, but Krane broke the silence instead.

"I didn't mean to get into a dissertation about this," Krane said. "I came to Japan because we're looking for a partner."

Toshio nodded, smiled approvingly, then reached back into the three years he had spent in junior high school English, the three years he had spent in high school English, and the other year or so he had accumulated in various

21

conversation classes since he started working. "Good timing," he said in English.

Krane appeared to be delighted and Tahara surprised.

"I think," Krane said, "that as Americans we may have given off an impression that we know it all. But we don't. We have a lot to learn."

Toshio nodded. Krane gave every appearance of sincerity. "America is a great country," Toshio said.

"And Japan is a great country," Krane said. "I'm very impressed with what I've seen. We could learn a lot. For one, we could stand to learn more about the Japanese management style."

It's not really the Japanese manager, Toshio thought, it's the Japanese worker. He noticed that Tahara was stifling a yawn. Maybe it is management, he thought.

"Why Diamond Advertising?" Toshio asked.

Krane smiled. "To tell you the truth," he said, "I wrote to you after finding your name in a directory."

"Really?" Toshio asked. "Which directory was that?"

Krane could not remember. "It'll come to me," he said.

"Isn't that something?" Toshio remarked. How did we lose the war? he wondered.

"Most of our clients are American companies who have had difficulty breaking into the Japanese market or who have yet to try," Krane said. "I'm here because we realize the whole process of sales and distribution in Japan is so different."

"What makes it different?" Tahara asked.

We don't buy from foreigners, Toshio thought. We prefer Japanese things.

"I wish I knew what made it different," Krane replied, "but this much I do know—even on this trip I've seen things American companies were doing that seem out of place."

"For example?" Toshio asked.

"I saw a McDonalds with an outdoor eating area," Krane said, "even though Japanese have a custom about not eating outdoors. Almost a taboo, am I right?"

"It's breaking down."

"And I saw an ad for Coca-Cola on television," Krane said, "that showed one individual drinking Coke by himself. Japanese tend toward the group, I thought. The commercial should have shown a whole group of people drinking Coke."

Toshio was impressed. Krane had not spent much time in Japan, but he seemed to have the right instincts. "You understand these things," Toshio said. "Why do you need a partner?"

"Not everything is this apparent," Krane said. "Tell me what you would do about this one. One of our clients makes fine lingerie and has been asking us for more than a year to help them develop a marketing plan for Japan. To be honest, we don't know where to begin. We don't know whether to recommend the same kind of newspaper and magazine advertising we do for them in the States, or whether we would be better off doing things differently. It's not enough to know that there's a difference between our two countries. You have to know what to do about it."

Toshio nodded.

"What would you do?" Krane asked.

The question caught Toshio off stride. "Very difficult," he said, sitting back in his chair to think.

But as had occasionally been the case during his career in advertising, Toshio spontaneously conceived and then visualized a campaign he was sure would be so stunning that he told himself he did not even need to see the product to know how successful his push would be. Toshio envisioned a campaign using high fashion models drinking Coca-Cola and eating at outdoor McDonalds' eating areas dressed in nothing more than this company's lingerie while a soft voice whispered in the background, "America, American, America. . . ."

Toshio decided to hold this one. But he was pleased with himself. He relished the thought he was already becoming an international expert in his field.

"I would have to know more about the situation before saying," Toshio answered. "Each client has different needs."

"Of course," Krane said and nodded.

The meeting seemed to lose its momentum. Twice Krane tried to introduce the particulars of how Sweet Wells worked with its affiliates. Each time he met a stony response.

"What are your plans from here?" Toshio asked.

"I'm going to Yokohama this afternoon," Krane said. "Tomorrow to Osaka."

"You're a busy man," Toshio said.

"Too busy," Krane replied, "but I'm glad we could meet. I'd like to keep in touch."

"By all means," Toshio said. "Please, please keep in touch."

"I brought some information on Sweet Wells," Krane said and opened his briefcase, "so you'll know more about our company."

Toshio accepted the various brochures and folders. "How are you traveling to Yokohama?" he asked.

"By train, I assume," Krane looked to his interpreter for guidance, "unless there's a better way."

Toshio grinned. He would drive Krane to Yokohama himself. Never mind that making arrangements and driving might take two, maybe three, times as long as going by train. Toshio wished to see Krane to his next destination personally.

"Just a minute," Toshio said. "Excuse me." He picked up the phone to dial. "Toshio," he spoke into the phone when Nozomi answered.

"Oh," she said, "it's you."

"Something has come up," he said. "I need the car. Can you bring it down here?"

"I'd like to," she said, "but it's in the shop."

Toshio smiled at his guests. "What's it doing there?" he asked.

"I took it in for maintenance."

"Why did you do that?"

"It said to in the book."

"Which book?"

"The one that came with the car."

"Nozomi," he said, "they don't print those things because they think you're going to follow them."

"Why do they print them then?"

Toshio laughed. "Nozomi," he said, "believe me, not because they think you're going to follow them."

"How do you know?"

"How do I know?" he asked. "Because I write them." He slammed down the phone. "My wife," Toshio apologized to Krane. "Tahara," he said, "you're not doing anything this afternoon, are you?"

"The girls from the modeling agency," Tahara said.

Toshio nodded. "Good," he said. "You see our guest to Yokohama. I'll keep an eye on things here."

"Tahara was going to Yokohama anyway," Toshio insisted over Krane's protest.

Tahara concurred.

"I'm sorry I can't offer you a ride," Toshio said. "My wife took the car into the shop." He shook his head.

"I appreciate your offer," Krane said. "I'm sure we'll be fine."

"Have you married?" Toshio asked.

Krane laughed. "Twice," he said. "Why?"

"Twice!" Toshio said.

"Twice," Krane said. "Does that seem strange? You have to understand. In America we make changes all the time. New job. New city. New family."

Toshio nodded. "In Japan," he replied, "same job, same city, same family."

TWO

"The Japanese farmer is a rich man," Hiroto Itoh said.

Toshio nodded. Itoh was getting older. One of the surest signs—he now freely transferred the authority he had earned in one area of his life, specifically business, to other areas in which he had less experience. Not that Itoh wasn't right in what he was saying, it was more the way he said it. The way he assumed that everyone would be interested.

"The farmer receives political protection," he said, "not because he needs it, but because he can demand it. He has land. He's wealthy, powerful."

Toshio nodded, on an automatic pilot of sorts. Itoh was drunk. Saeki too. After an afternoon at the sumo matches they had invited Toshio to join them at one of Itoh's favorite, most exclusive restaurants. The men occupied a small, private room upstairs. Toshio sat cross-legged on the matted tatami floor across from Itoh. Saeki, fighting to hold his head up, leaned back against the wall. Saeki was a poor drinker—an unfortunate handicap. In the business world, Toshio knew, one's liver was often more important than one's brain.

27

"Why doesn't the government reapportion the districts?" Itoh asked. "We elect our parliament from the same districts we've used since the war. Why? Because the party protects the farmers, who protect the party, who protects the farmers. And why do I bring this up?" He paused for effect. "Because of one firmly held belief." He cleared his throat. "It's not people who change, but nations. Nations change."

Toshio did not like politics. Neither did he care for this kind of conversation. Business entertainment had become more and more of a chore lately. What happened to the days, he wondered, when all he had to do was get drunk and laid?

Itoh offered Toshio a Mild Seven, one of the many brands packaged to look like their foreign competition. Toshio accepted. He moved to offer Itoh a light, but reaching into his pocket for his lighter his mind wandered. He thought about the models who had passed through his office just an hour or two before. The one model in particular, Yuko. He tried to remember her full name. Itoh's politics could not dampen the anticipation this girl had created for Toshio. The anxiety. And maybe it wasn't even the girls. Toshio knew only this: in a way he had no longer considered possible, something was happening.

Toshio felt like changing the subject. He wanted to discuss his first meeting with the American, Ted Krane. Or talk business, maybe sports. Anything else. "Business conditions sure seem good," he said quickly.

It was an uncharacteristic statement, a departure from the pessimistic stance almost uniformly taken. Toshio recognized his mistake at once. This was not a conversation among equals such that he could have with Ken Kondo. Itoh was an important man. His superior. As owner of Japan's largest privately-held septic tank clean-up company, Itoh controlled a small empire from the trailer he called his office.

Toshio's outburst had not been missed. "Business should be good," Itoh said. "What else are people doing around here?"

A hostess attired in a kimono opened the rice paper-covered door and approached the table on her knees. "More sake?" she asked.

"More sake," Itoh responded, "and bring us something to eat."

Saeki stirred against the wall, then burped and leaned forward. Toshio was afraid Saeki might throw up. "He's a good man, Matsuzaka," Itoh put his hand on Saeki's shoulder and squeezed, "easy to work with."

Toshio smiled. Saeki was a good man—hardworking and loyal. Toshio felt relieved with Itoh's words, almost happy. He hoped he would never make the mistake of under-estimating Itoh. Toshio had seen the signs. Itoh held a reserve inside, a strength known as basement power.

Itoh took a drag on his cigarette. "You know anything about politics, Matsuzaka?"

Toshio knew one thing. He knew he hated being disturbed by campaign workers who drove around in cars before elections shouting slogans into earsplitting loud-speaker systems.

"I know what you're thinking," Itoh said, "and I don't pretend to be an expert. What I knew about politics three or four years ago . . . I knew there was one party, and I knew that we gave to the party. A business expense. . . ." He made a fist. "You rarely see the benefits, but try and live without it." He slammed his fist into the palm of his other hand. "It's not just in construction. . . ." He leaned over, bloated; blood vessels marked tracks on his nose.

Toshio's vision fixed on Itoh's earlobes. They were enormous, fleshy and fat. If, as folklore had it, such large earlobes really did indicate a predisposition toward wealth, then Itoh's success had indeed been clearly destined. Toshio had wondered what Itoh would do with his money. The answer was becoming apparent.

"Politics, Matsuzaka," he said, "what do you think?"

Their hostess slid the door open again. She set a dish of sashimi in front of each man and poured more sake. Each dish of sashimi was garnished with a small yellow flower.

"Kanpai!" Toshio said, holding up his glass. Cheers!

"Kanpai!" Saeki said.

"Kanpai!" Itoh said. The men drank, then filled each other's cups to drink again.

"Itadakimasu," Toshio added. I am receiving.

The food seemed to quiet the men. Each became more and more absorbed—perhaps even momentarily at peace—in his own world. Itoh conducting affairs of state. Toshio affairs. Saeki himself.

Dinner passed quickly. Toshio lost the obligatory fight afterwards as to who would pay when Itoh had the bill put on his account with the restaurant. Just as well, Toshio thought, the cost of entertainment lately. . . . He looked at Saeki. Doesn't the man ever eat at home? he wondered.

Toshio stipulated that Diamond Advertising would pay the next out, but did not take up too much time insisting. He knew that Itoh would want to catch the 9:15. Itoh always took the 9:15.

Saeki hailed a cab and insisted with Toshio that they accompany Itoh to the station. Toshio had expected Itoh to take the 9:15 from the moment Saeki had called to relay the invitation. Toshio made it a point to know his friends' and associates' schedules as intimately as possible. With people so busy and life so organized it was a necessity, one of the first things to find out about someone. If schedules did not line up it would be difficult to promote a relationship. Toshio made adjustments accordingly.

With Itoh this wasn't difficult. Regardless of what plans they had made, "Dinner was sure good," he would say. "I'll have to come back to the city when I can spend more time." On to the 9:15. Invariably. But return he would. Toshio knew that Itoh felt safe with Saeki, safe with Diamond Advertising. Exploring dreams of glory over drinks in the city, Itoh could ramble as he pleased. As for tomorrow— sober at the operating facility—tomorrow was an early start. Another day and business as usual.

Saeki ran ahead to buy platform tickets. Toshio and Itoh followed at a more leisurely, but still businesslike pace. Toshio felt sometimes like he had spent half his life in train stations. So many comings and goings, a little bit sad. There was nothing particularly welcoming about train stations in and of themselves. But they were clean and safe. The trains ran on time.

Toshio and Saeki waited for Itoh's train to depart before leaving themselves. Itoh took a window seat and appeared tired but content. Occasionally he would look directly at Toshio and Saeki. Then Saeki would bow or Saeki and Toshio would bow almost together. Toshio knew there were just a few minutes before the train would leave; he refused whatever urge he had to look at his watch or any of the station clocks. He and Saeki would wait as long as was necessary.

The train pulled out promptly at 9:15. Toshio and Saeki bowed one more time and then waved until they were sure Itoh was out of sight.

Toshio turned to face an intoxicated Saeki. What time he had before his meeting at Esprit he did not feel like killing with Saeki.

"I think that some of the men were planning to meet at Applause," Toshio said. Applause was a bar the salarymen frequented. "Please tell them I'm tied up and can't make it."

"Understood," Saeki said, having received his release. He could go to Applause where he might, in fact, meet some of his colleagues, or he could call it a day. He had done his bit. Toshio obviously had other matters to attend.

"If you can find a way," Saeki said, "I know the men at Applause would be happy to see you."

"I'll try," Toshio responded and said good-bye. Cooperation at the office was important, but not that important.

Toshio walked out to the street and found himself heading toward an area rife with "pink salons." These bars served more than drinks. Toshio told himself he would not go in. It was too early and he felt uncomfortable by himself. He just felt like walking around, loosening up.

Toshio studied the girls he passed on the street. He wondered which girls were going home, which girls would marry, which girls were married, which girls worked for money. The pink salons sported posters of the most popular young female singers. "Young girls inside," the hustlers said. "Students." Toshio tried to look relaxed. Suddenly he felt foolish roaming around by himself. Like he was hounding. He hoped he wouldn't run into anybody he knew.

Toshio decided it would be better to kill a little time playing *pachinko*. There was a parlor nearby. He could walk.

It was smoky inside. Many seats were available along the walls, but only a few at Toshio's favorite game, "Fever." Toshio exchanged several thousand-yen notes for steel balls. As he looked around to see the other people—mostly men— he felt slightly ashamed that he still went in for this sort of thing.

Background military march music played loudly over the sound of machines and steel balls and the occasional voices of men exchanging their balls at the counter for cigarettes or candy or for plastic markers to be taken across the street and redeemed for money. Toshio looked for an available machine whose built-in ashtray was full. The key to winning at *pachinko* was to find the right machine. Presumably a machine whose ashtray was full was a machine where someone had been able to sit for awhile. Toshio found his ashtray and sat down.

Fever had a special feature. In addition to winning balls by having a live ball work its way into certain areas of the board, there was also the possibility of activating a casino element to the game. A three digit number would be electronically displayed and if 333 or 777 came up, everything moved to a bonus round where automatic flippers came into play as well as a large extra collector in the middle of the board. Then from ten minutes to a half hour or so, balls came pouring out—kind of a *pachinko* heaven. Toshio had achieved this jackpot twice. It didn't really involve that much money, but he liked the feeling. There were worse ways to spend time, he told himself, and he was always improving. In fact, sometimes Toshio felt he could see much larger things through *pachinko,* more important things that made it that much more worthwhile.

Toshio had a hard time getting a feel for the particular machine he had chosen. He expected a brief sacrifice period during which he would experiment to develop a sense of the machine, but not until he had lost most of his balls did he begin to trade with the machine over minor awards that kept him alive. A young man wearing extraordinarily thick glasses took a temporarily vacant seat next to his and Toshio noticed that his machine displayed a 767 before long. But 767 had no meaning and there didn't seem to be much action around. Toshio knew the machines could be adjusted in order to make it harder for customers to win.

Suddenly, a 333 lit up on the lady's machine two spaces over. Immediately one of the workers came running over with a large plastic container for the overflow balls that would soon be pouring out. On his way this worker inadvertently knocked into Toshio with an elbow and either did not realize what he had done or did not care to apologize. Toshio could see the man was Korean. It wasn't always easy to tell, but in the context of a *pachinko* parlor, Toshio was sure. Koreans seemed to own most of them. Toshio now felt acutely aware of their presence around him. The man who had run into him was standing and laughing with another employee. They might as well have been laughing at him. Toshio did not like Koreans. Especially these Koreans who tried to assimilate, who took on Japanese names and worked to build up their businesses. It was too bad they didn't all go home. Toshio had nothing to do with the occupation of the mainland. Now if Japanese authorities wanted to overlook background checks on potential salarymen or wanted to fingerprint Koreans still living in Japan, that was fine. The peoples were like two bad brothers, Toshio thought, and the issue was simple. He did not like them.

Toshio returned his attention to the machine. The red light was blinking at intervals, balls were discharging. He watched the upward arc of each ball, sometimes losing it in the middle of the board with the flight of the next ball. When the red light came on he traced the spent balls' paths to see which one had done the job. Over and over the machine sent balls through a trajectory in its sky. Over and over they fell uncontrollably to their fate. Two spaces over the woman's machine quieted and she carried her container of balls to the counter for exchange. Over and over Toshio watched balls shooting up and then falling down. When his luck ran out he

34

washed his hands at the sink by the door and walked out into the street.

Checking his watch, Toshio could see that he had overstayed with the *pachinko*. He hurried over to Esprit afraid to be late, but at the same time knowing Ozaki would surely keep him waiting. An invitation from Shun Ozaki was more or less a command performance, the arrangements too well understood to make excuses later. And with the Big Catch advertising debacle upon him, Toshio could not risk appearing to steal a few minutes by arriving late, as earlier he could not have risked lobbying for another meeting place. When Ozaki finally did arrive, when he would ask the hostess how long Toshio had been waiting, every minute more was a point Toshio needed toward earning his redemption.

Esprit held fifteen guests at capacity. Between the *mama-san*, Chiho, her two hostesses, Toshio, and the other party of three men—well on their way to a good drunk, the bar was already looking comfortably occupied.

One other employee stopped by every hour for twenty minutes or so to play guitar. This guitarist worked for Esprit and he worked for another snack in the building as well. The easiest way to operate as a club without a license was to serve food or snacks—hence the word "snack."

Toshio looked at the three men across the room who were drinking heavily and trying to impress one of the hostesses. Toshio thought again about the scene with Itoh and Saeki at the train station and then he took a long, hard look at Chiho who, standing in the corner placing an order for food over the telephone, did not know she was being watched. Seeing her again like this reminded Toshio she was still a young woman and, he could not deny it, attractive too.

A snack has several purposes. The first is to make a businessman feel important. The second is to provide an alternative to going home. And the third is to provide a convenient way of channeling corporate funds to the *mama-san* who was sometimes a mistress to one of her corporate clients. By going often and entertaining lavishly, a corporate bigwig could create an income for his mistress through the company expense account. Toshio knew these things were true. Intimately.

One of the hostesses brought Toshio a hot napkin and unrolled it for him so he could wash his hands. Toshio put it over his face instead, as if to steam out the less agreeable parts of the day.

"That's sure a lot of perfume you're wearing," he said to the girl.

She took his hand towel away and disappeared into the bathroom. The other girl appeared soon after with two small dishes of food and a beer. One of the dishes contained a kind of steamed green beans still in the pod. The other, which Toshio surveyed in his boredom, held fourteen smoked almonds and eleven M&M's. The hostess poured Toshio's beer, but then took a seat with Chiho at the other men's table. Chiho had greeted Toshio briefly on his entrance. Toshio did not like Esprit anymore and under circumstances other than these would surely have avoided it.

Shun Ozaki arrived about fifty minutes late with two of his cohorts. His timing was less than ideal. With an open beer in front of him, not enough time had passed for Toshio to joke about not having been able to wait to start drinking. But then neither had he waited. Chiho and the hostesses had not been much help, but the mistake was his own. A stupid mistake. Toshio stood up to greet the man who was in effect his benefactor, but Ozaki was already taken up with Chiho. Chiho had come running over immediately, not a difficult feat, since in the tiny bar she was only two steps away. Toshio resented the way she greeted Ozaki. She had worked at Diamond Advertising once. Toshio had helped her. For a while they had a thing. Away from her now it didn't bother him, but seeing her like this was unpleasant.

Toshio reminded himself what a lousy secretary Chiho had been, never very effective in the office even when she tried. He thought about how much more Mitsue could do. Mitsue was no beauty, but she did know how to dig in. Toshio had seen Mitsue move to the copying machine when she knew another girl was trying to get there at the same time. Toshio thought it was funny. Mitsue was aggressive with the copying machine. Chiho had merely been aggressive. Never right for the office. Even in company uniform, standing with the other girls, she looked different. Distracted. He had tried to overlook it. Cheap.

He learned his lesson. Chiho had been his first newly hired employee. She volunteered regularly to stay late. She didn't do much, but she did hang around. He liked that. She was always smiling, always seemed to be bringing tea or something into his office. It was nice. A help, a plus. One night finding themselves alone in the office Toshio opened up. He talked about his fears regarding the company's prospects, about his occasional headaches, his fatigue. She offered to massage. He was surprised. And then he was surprised how easy it was. That he was taking her right on the floor.

Toshio went crazy for this girl. He sought the relief and release she afforded whenever he could isolate her. Each meeting became that much more exciting by the delays involved and by the difficulties in getting together and the pressure and the need to hide the affair from his employees and his wife.

But then the relationship changed. He didn't know why. Chiho became more passive, less interested. She wouldn't help him to undress her and she never moved to undress him. He tried to please her. Always he asked what she liked. About food, clothing, music, sex. "I dislike it all," she said. So it was his suggestion she should leave. Instead of the office she could work in a snack. After some time had passed—when she knew the business better and when people would be less likely to talk—he would set her up with her own snack. But she seemed to understand the business from the beginning; she made him give her the money before leaving.

Chiho went back for a bottle of whiskey, Ozaki's personal bottle of whiskey, returned to their table and began paying close attention to Toshio as well as to the other men. Toshio hated this, the way she played to him now, with Ozaki there. Toshio hated the way he felt around Shun Ozaki in general. True, Ozaki had been a godfather to Toshio over the years in business, but at a price on a personal basis. Tonight Ozaki had not even bothered to ask how long he had kept Toshio waiting. It was his way of keeping Toshio's nose in the thick of it. Ozaki would not mention the advertising campaign tonight, would not let on as to consequences or necessary changes. He would just maintain a certain level of tension in a setting he knew made Toshio uncomfortable.

As if she were fulfilling destiny, Chiho put ice into their glasses and then added whiskey and water . The whole thing made Toshio feel like he would rather drink his beer.

"Matsuzaka?"

Toshio looked up to see the men holding their glasses. He felt like picking up his beer instead—doing something different to spite Ozaki.

"Matsuzaka?" Ozaki repeated.

Toshio looked at the whiskey and water that was waiting and somehow in the reflection noticed his balance sheet, income statement, sources and uses, client list and appointment book. Better to drink.

"Kanpai!" Toshio lifted his glass to say. Ozaki ignored him for most of the rest of the evening, fawning over Chiho and spilling his drink. Toshio had introduced Ozaki to Esprit, joking at the time about Chiho having her own club. He didn't know if the others knew—although they must have known—about their relationship. He didn't take his salarymen to Esprit, even then they usually went to Applause. But he did take his clients. Ozaki had flipped for Chiho immediately. In retrospect it was easy to see what had happened between Ozaki and Chiho. She had moved quickly, Toshio could see it now. He had been the fool.

Chiho excused herself and then walked over to total the check for the men who had begun earlier. Toshio could overhear their conversation. The bill was astonishing. For a second he felt envious Chiho could make so much money doing so little. It didn't seem fair. Snacks were boring, their prices arbitrary.

Toshio moved to the guitarist's empty seat. Esprit had a *karaoke* sound system on which customers could sing popular songs over background music recorded without vocals. Toshio liked *karaoke* and fancied himself a pretty good singer. He made the few Western songs his specialty to create a certain mystique, having discovered that with a touch of bravura in his performance everybody assumed he knew what he was doing.

He liked to sing behind the beat. Slowly. Not so the music ever appeared to be leading, but to add a little tension, occasionally a feeling of sadness. As for the songs themselves, Toshio wished there were more English language numbers. Along with the hundreds and hundreds

39

of Japanese songs, only ten or twelve Western songs were usually included: "Yesterday," "Country Road," "When The Saints Come Marching In," "The Impossible Dream," "New York, New York." Toshio's all-time favorite was "(I Did It) My Way." He saved it for last. The only thing Toshio didn't like about "My Way" was that it seemed to be every salaryman's favorite.

Toshio looked at Ozaki and Chiho who were talking while he was singing. Ozaki seemed to lose his hearing when he was drunk. He and Chiho were practically shouting at each other to be understood. Toshio had to sing over their yelling. Toshio felt like a doormat now and suddenly singing a song in English that nobody could understand did not seem so great; it captured the way he felt, the sense of being an outsider. He wanted to see Kondo. A friend. He would hold on until Ozaki left and then he would look for Kondo.

Everyone applauded when Toshio finished. Chiho filled his glass, Ozaki directed a little attention his way. Toshio wondered if he had been too harsh with his thoughts. One of Ozaki's friends asked him questions about where he had grown up, about his family, his children. Toshio didn't know which he liked least, being left on the outside or having to answer this man's questions. But then the man got up to sing and Toshio found Chiho sitting next to him. Ozaki was drunk, Chiho had been drinking too. Toshio felt her body next to his own. Her body dug into his body. Why hadn't he been stronger before, acted to keep her? And why did he let her lean against him now as if he could forgive her?

He thought about one time he had taken her, a moment he had thought about many times. They had fallen asleep and when he woke up afterwards he found himself sprawled head on the floor beneath her legs spread apart. She was wearing a bra and an unbuttoned blouse. That was all. He

40

was completely naked. They had been drunk and the clearest thing he could remember was that they had made it. That much he could remember. He had come hard. He always did with Chiho. Even when she wouldn't touch him. Even when she would say it was no good when he would want to meet, no good when he was undressing her, no good when he was about to enter her. But she never left and she never made him stop. And she never said that it was no good afterwards. Drunk on the floor that night he looked up between her legs as she was sleeping. What was it? he asked himself.

"You never come here anymore," Chiho said.

It was painful for Toshio to hear. On the slight chance she was really asking him to come around, he could not respond the way he wanted to, not with Ozaki there. And on the more likely chance she was teasing him, he could not respond the way he wanted to either. She could take her snack and Ozaki too. They were perfect for each other. Anyway, how many times had girls in snacks asked him to come back? It was a come on, what kept the snack open. Most of the time the girls didn't even use their real names. Just the other night he had asked a girl for her phone number. "123-4567," she said.

Ozaki was ready to leave. Chiho all of a sudden was helping him on with his coat. Now saying good-bye to Toshio as well. Pushing Toshio out with the group.

Toshio stumbled out onto the street. He saw Ozaki and his friends to separate cabs and then decided to look for Kondo at On The Rocks, another snack and Kondo's favorite hangout. Toshio considered calling, but he liked the possibility of surprising Kondo better. He was glad to know Kondo, someone he could laugh with, not for or at. Most of the relationships he had to contend with involved some sort of hierarchy and position. Someone to bow to in some sense, or vice-versa. Friendships among equals were much rarer, hard to find.

Kondo was holding court when Toshio walked in. Toshio did not know exactly what Kondo was talking about, but he could guess the general direction. In addition to Kondo there was a younger salaryman named Noguchi whom Toshio had seen before and who seemed to be working at acting relaxed. There were also four girls around in various stages of either sitting with the men, straightening things up or going in and out of the bathroom. The girls were giggling a lot and, if a little tired, actually seemed to be interested in what Kondo was saying.

Kondo looked like a guy with a crooked penis, Toshio could not help thinking whenever they met. His travel firm specialized in pleasure trips for men throughout the Orient. On Toshio's suggestion the brochures had once been titled, "Safari in Search of Oasis." On the suggestion of the Foreign Ministry the brochures were now headed, "Golfing Vacations in Asia." His brother had called with the news.

Another phone call Toshio would never forget came from a Filipino girl he had once met "on safari" in Manila. Without thinking, he had given her his business card and invited her to visit him in Japan. Toshio had never expected she would. Kondo had saved the day when she did. Kondo put the girl up in a hotel, sent her on a tour of the city and then whisked her out of town. It had cemented the friendship—Kondo's and Toshio's, that is. Kondo did not fall all over himself when Toshio walked in the door. He just moved over to make a place for him. Toshio felt comfortable, didn't care that he probably looked a mess or was drunk already.

Kondo was talking about his last trip. A week in Mexico with a stopover on the way back in Los Angeles. Kondo said it was the last time he would lead a group to North

America if he could help it. The men had all come down with diarrhea by the time they had left Los Angeles.

"They say the United States has become a service economy," he said. "What kind of service are they talking about?"

"And you have to leave money for a tip," Noguchi said, "or they get mad."

"That's right," Kondo nodded. "Now cover your ears," he said to the girls at the table. He waited until they were pretending to before he would continue. "We say, 'Go,' "but they say, 'Come.'"

Toshio had heard this before.

"I don't understand," one of the girls said.

"In sex," Kondo explained, "they say, 'I'm coming, I'm coming,' when we say, 'I'm going.'"

"No!" she said.

"Yes!" he said.

"Then did you come?" she asked. "Or did you go?"

"I came and I went," Kondo laughed.

"I don't think you know how to have sex in English," she said.

The hostesses at On The Rocks were not very pretty, but they were pretty naughty. Toshio looked around the room. Of the four girls, he had not seen one before. Another, he had heard, was gay. And of the other two, Toshio had made it with one and had a clear chance but chose not to with the other, which was just as well because Kondo had said he had started poking her regularly not long afterwards.

"What was Mexico like?" one of the girls asked. Toshio remembered she called herself Eve. "Any funny stories?"

"You might appreciate this one," Kondo said to Toshio, as if it were too difficult for the others. "People try very hard to please you there. They don't like to disappoint you with an answer by saying, 'I don't know.' When we first arrived

43

Mexico I asked a man if the time difference between Los Angeles and Mexico City was two hours or three hours. He didn't know. 'Maybe two and a half,' he said."

Nobody laughed.

"No funny stories then," Kondo said.

"Come now!" Eve said.

"I'd like to," Kondo said, making a thrusting motion with his hips.

"That's not what I meant," she said. "I just thought you probably had another story."

"But not a funny story," Kondo said, "a serious story. Did I tell you we took a mule team out on an overnight trip?"

She shook her head no.

"We were running late and it got dark very suddenly. To make things worse—there were so many guides I don't know how it happened—one of the men and I got separated from the group. We were lost. Then our mules wouldn't move. Out of frustration I started jumping up and down shouting, 'Move, you ass! Move!' I was screaming, but my ass wouldn't move. Finally I got off and damn if we weren't standing right on the edge of a cliff. That mule saved my life."

"It's a good thing mules don't speak Japanese," Toshio said.

"Mexico sounds like a strange place," Noguchi added when they stopped laughing. "To be honest, it scares me." Toshio looked at this guy. Noguchi had no business connections with Kondo. He looked like a regular salaryman, he acted like a regular salaryman, he was a regular salaryman. But where was Noguchi's group? Toshio had only seen him alone or with Kondo—never with his office colleagues or clients.

"What about Mexican . . ." Noguchi mouthed the word.

"My God," Kondo feigned dramatically, "in front of the women like that?"

"They don't care," Noguchi said.

Kondo would have dropped it.

"Do you mind?" Noguchi asked one of the girls.

Kondo seesawed with him for a few minutes, but Noguchi persisted.

"Sideways," Kondo said finally.

"Well," Toshio said and stood up. But for a second he was afraid he might pass out. He tried to fix his attention on the microphone stand.

"Easier for us," Kondo said. "You can breathe."

Noguchi laughed.

Kondo winked at one of the girls. "I'm starving," he said. "Let's get something to eat, huh? *Okonomiyaki.*"

When On The Rocks closed up Noguchi disappeared. Toshio didn't know where. "That's the problem with younger people," Kondo said. "Every time they see two people making love in the movies, they see two people in bed. They have no imagination." Toshio liked the idea of going out with Kondo and the girls. Five girls now. Toshio wasn't sure where the other girl came from. On The Rocks was a looser snack than most. It seemed to have an absentee *mama-san.*

Toshio looked behind as he was going out the door. There was so little there. A few chairs and tables. A bar. The *karaoke* system. Nothing good ever comes out of a snack, he thought.

The group stopped in front of the *okonomiyaki* shop to look at the imitation food displayed in a case mounted against the building. Sometimes people looked at these displays to see what food a restaurant served or to check on prices, but sometimes people paused simply to marvel at how lifelike the imitation food really was.

45

In the case of this shop, however, Toshio already knew what they would order. The reason they stood around the display case was that the modeled food had been there too long and the colors were turning. Reds were browning, greens were yellowing and the whites were dusty. The group stood and laughed about this until they laughed that they had chosen to eat there. Finally the cold drove them in.

The shop was a little dirty in the corners. Toshio had seen cockroaches there before. Grease had a tendency to come shooting off the grill. Everything about *okonomiyaki* said mess. From the stirring and pouring to the final presentation, *okonomiyaki* could be described as many things, but not as attractive. However fresh the ingredients might be they were all fried into one general taste, the final product a kind of pizza-pancake. Toshio ate his *okonomiyaki* with a touch of mayonnaise. Other foods might taste better, but *okonomiyaki* was what he wanted. Kondo ordered beers all around.

Toshio and the girls took the metal containers of *okonomiyaki* ingredients to stir and then fry on the griddle in front of them as soon as they were brought to the table. As much as Toshio liked Kondo, there was something he had learned through the course of their friendship. Kondo did not make *okonomiyaki* very well. He didn't stir it long enough and he didn't cook it evenly. Worse still, he went heavy with the sweet sauce.

It was close to two o'clock. Toshio liked the feeling of sitting with Kondo and all the girls on the tatami with the food cooking and splattering around them. These were Japanese girls. He felt comfortable. He could relax. Toshio had been with Kondo in some crazy situations. Maybe this wasn't as wild as being sucked off by fifteen year-olds in Thailand, but it sure felt more secure. He looked at Kondo digging into his *okonomiyaki*. Toshio knew a secret. The samurai were not all great men.

The *okonomiyaki* sat like ballast in Toshio's stomach. His head didn't feel much clearer, but he might have been a little steadier on his feet. If he could stand up. Toshio decided it was time to make the move home. If it was just Kondo and himself with two of the girls he might have hung around. With all five of the girls there he knew he would have to wait until the group split up. Even then he could not be sure. Maybe they would all go home at once. Or three girls could be left at the end. Toshio did not like odd numbers.

Kondo had more time to kill. Not that Toshio had to return, but maybe something was tugging. Kondo had never married, a rarity and condition that alternatively called out both feelings of pity and jealousy from Toshio. People who get laid a lot, Toshio knew, can stay up all night and will sleep with anybody. They stay up all night even in the most boring and unpromising circumstances. Kondo was a prime example. But looking and even knowing how little he would have to do for any of these girls—when Toshio thought about having to sit there for the other hour or two or three it would take until they all got tired and split up—when he and which one would go to a "love hotel" so as anonymously to get in and out of a room set up with one thing and only one thing in mind. . . . When Toshio thought about staying awake and talking to these girls for another hour or two he decided he would rather not. In that moment he didn't envy Kondo. He felt like going home.

Kondo tried to drag Toshio down, to tackle him as Toshio got up to pay the bill. "Let's drink some more," he said.

"I'd like to," Toshio said, "But I . . ." it was hard to say ". . . need to go home."

The whole party got up to see Toshio out to the street where taxis waited in line to take the businessmen home who had missed their last trains. Toshio hoped he wouldn't get a talkative driver. He wanted to sleep.

Everyone waved good-bye. In the car Toshio tried to remember the names of all five of the girls and then he fell asleep.

Although there was virtually no traffic and they were traveling through flat areas, the driver pulled the emergency brake at every stop. Toshio woke up. "Are we rolling down a hill?" he asked.

The driver stopped with the emergency. Toshio went back to sleep. When the driver woke him again, Toshio looked at the meter and knew that the driver had not taken advantage of him, had not taken a longer route. Toshio began to give more specific instructions, but to his surprise noticed that the neighborhood driving range, where he sometimes practiced, was apparently still open. What the hell.

"This is fine," he said and paid the driver, who was wearing white gloves.

Toshio approached the driving range, a small affair bounded by nets and high fences. Although the lights had been left on, no one was there. Toshio was annoyed with himself. He felt stupid. He would walk the rest of the way home. The streets were practically empty. Occasionally a taxi but no passersby. Toshio did not like walking alone at night—a thing about ghosts.

Approaching the block before their house Toshio's thoughts turned to Nozomi. He thought about how sometimes when she was unhappy she would put things indirectly and how she always seemed to know the one word or phrase in a situation that could most irritate him. He hoped she wouldn't be up.

Then he hoped she would be up. He felt like tagging her.

Then he hoped she would be asleep. That's what he wanted himself. To go to sleep.

48

There was a light on in the house. As usual. He couldn't tell, maybe she was awake. Maybe not. He looked at his watch. The hands spun toward him. He was drunk. Be quiet, he thought coming up to the house, don't wake the children.

He hoped she was asleep. And if not, he wondered what she would say.

He slid the door open.

"Welcome home," she said.

THREE

Nozomi was weathering a strange uneasiness. The children were in school. Toshio was at the office. Nozomi could not fight the realization any longer that so much of her time was now spent waiting. Waiting for deliveries. Waiting for the phone to ring. Waiting for the children.

Wednesday was "little garbage day," held weekly to pick up the usual household garbage. Heavier garbage was collected once a month on "big garbage day," when TV sets, stereos, appliances and furniture would sometimes be left on the street, abandoned because of a general aversion to used things. On a little garbage day like today, however, only mounds of black and blue plastic garbage bags waited for pick-up.

Nozomi knew that maintaining a household in the past had been a continuing occupation. Shopping and preparing the food was almost a full-time job in itself. No kitchen appliances in the past. No appliances to help clean the house or do the laundry. Nozomi could understand the time required to maintain a household then. She had seen how her own mother worked. But how long did it take to keep a house now? Washing machine, vacuum cleaner, refrigerator, rice maker. The family had just purchased a coffee maker with its own grinder. How ridiculous was that? The companies had nearly completed their improvement—and invasion—of her world. How successfully had she been able to enter theirs?

She looked at her watch. Why concern yourself with this now? she thought. There were many things to do. The fish market. She needed tofu. The beer would be delivered, but she should pick up for Toshio at the cleaners. The children wanted milk, the post office closed at five. If there was time, she should stop at the electrician's.

The weather was cold and wet. Humid as usual. Even being winter, humid. She walked out onto the street. What did you do this morning? she asked herself as she angled her umbrella to press across the street. Stop at the bank too. You're moving so slowly.

She paused by a building along the way. It's not summer fatigue in January, she thought. Her figure reflected against the building's mirrored glass. She looked so different at different times. Especially her eyes. Still attractive—thanks to what, she didn't know. Even pretty. But to judge yourself by a reflection off a bank building? she thought. Don't do it.

When she turned back to the street, Nozomi perceived a slightly familiar blur—something about the way it moved.

"Don't you recognize me?" People were so bundled up it was hard to make them out. "Don't make me stand here. Let's get some coffee." It was Reiko Higashi, a friend Nozomi had met some years ago when taking tennis lessons.

"Time . . ." Nozomi began.

"Time," Reiko laughed and took Nozomi's arm. "Don't worry so much."

As much as Nozomi could like Reiko, there was still something about her that made Nozomi nervous. It wasn't anything Reiko had done that embarrassed Nozomi. At least not yet. It was more the way she acted. Like a girl who won't admit to what she really wants.

Reiko pointed the way.

"*Irasshaimase,*" the owner said when they entered. Welcome.

"Two coffees," Reiko called out. Nozomi knew she was a regular.

Nozomi looked around. The coffee shop was empty. Even at capacity it would have held only ten or twelve people. She eyed the little bottles of red Tabasco sauce and the taller green containers of Parmesan cheese on each of the tables.

"I want to open a place," Reiko said.

Nozomi had heard this many times.

"I know what you're thinking," Reiko continued, "but not like this one."

Nozomi motioned for Reiko to keep her voice down. She was so rude.

"I want to open a cafe bar," she said, "a bigger place that serves drinks too."

"It's so much work," Nozomi said. "You'll have to be there every night until ten-thirty or eleven. Sometimes you won't get home until after midnight."

"Good," Reiko said, "because I'm not planning one for the front of my house. I don't want to be home before midnight."

The coffee was served with two miniature stainless steel pitchers of milk. Nozomi added sugar. Coffee made her feel differently. She liked the haze.

"Katsuichiro is putting up the money." Reiko's husband was a slow-talking, big-smile personality. The first time Nozomi had met him she thought he must be running all over town. He might humor Reiko about putting up the money, but she would never get it from him. Reiko had talked about it for months. Layout, menu, location, everything. "Did you mention joining in to Toshio?"

Nozomi said she would discuss it with him to be polite, but who puts money into something like that? And what if her husband said yes? That would be the worst thing. To be working outside the house didn't seem right. "Circumstances," she answered. "I'd like to, but circumstances are a little difficult."

Reiko understood. Nozomi would not be a partner.

"So much to do," Nozomi said.

"More coffee," Reiko ordered.

"Can't," Nozomi said.

"Why not? What else are you doing today?"

Nozomi thought about her list. There was actually some milk left in the house. The beer would be delivered. She needed fish, tofu. The dry cleaners and the post office would be open tomorrow. She could telephone the electrician. "I have to go to the fish market," she said.

"We'll go together."

It was hard to argue. Nozomi spent so much time alone these days. They paid the check and pulled on their overcoats.

The fish market was not far. Even in the cold, shopkeepers greeted them as they walked by. Some were friendlier than others.

"They're only friendly when you buy," Reiko said.

Nozomi laughed. "That's not true."

"No?" They were still laughing when they entered the store. "Look at Akiko," Reiko said. "Why did she have her hair permed like that?" Akiko was a younger, short, round woman who was trying to shop while carrying one child and watching another. Reiko noticed what Akiko was buying. "Octopus?"

Nozomi took Akiko's baby. "What's wrong with octopus?" Nozomi could understand Reiko's impatience with Akiko, but she thought her reaction was immature.

Akiko's other child, a daughter named Yukari, came running across the store to stand next to Nozomi.

"I'm so glad you're here," Akiko said. "The children have been awful all day."

"They're getting so big now," Nozomi observed.

Yukari beamed.

Akiko smiled. From the time Akiko had met Nozomi in their high school English club she knew Nozomi was special. The way she acted, the things she said, the way she took care of herself. Akiko's single wish through high school had been to wake up one morning and find she was Nozomi herself. Knowing that wasn't likely, Akiko had contented herself with association through their club. She had not expected friendship. Older girls didn't often take younger girls as friends. Besides, what did Akiko have to offer? She was short and heavy, she had bad skin and she could hardly manage a conversation. Even as they had gotten to know each other Akiko had been prepared for Nozomi to cut her off. It would have been natural.

"I need tuna," Nozomi said.

"For dinner?" Akiko asked.

"I like to have it for Toshio," she said. "Tonight I promised Sanae I would fix macaroni with white sauce."

"Macaroni with white sauce?" Yukari asked.

"Yes," Nozomi said, "don't you like it?"

"I really like it, but we never have it."

Akiko laughed. "Yukari, we had it last night."

"But it was a long time before that."

"Macaroni is her favorite," Akiko said. "I think she would eat it every night, wouldn't you, Yukari? It's macaroni now. Before that it was pizza toast. What was it before that,

Yukari? Spaghetti?" Akiko turned toward Nozomi. "Is something wrong?"

"No," Nozomi answered. "Why?"

"I don't know," Akiko said. "For a second you looked so, I don't know, distracted."

"Why doesn't Yukari come to our house for dinner?" Nozomi responded. "You can pick her up later."

"But she just had macaroni last night," Akiko said. "Besides, it's too much trouble."

"No trouble," Nozomi said.

"Really," Akiko said, "it's too much trouble."

"No trouble, I'm sure."

Akiko and Yukari stood looking gratefully at Nozomi as if frozen in the middle of the store. It was almost four. Sanae would be home soon, Nozomi thought. She might be home already. "Let's get some fish and go home."

"Right," Akiko said.

Nozomi handed Akiko her baby and shopped quickly. She found Reiko, who had wandered out of disinterest, and said good-bye. Then Nozomi reconfirmed her plans with Akiko and walked home with Yukari.

Sanae was standing in front of the house with two of her girlfriends. Just the sight of Sanae embarrassed Nozomi that she had been complaining to herself earlier in the day. Sanae brought these feelings out in Nozomi like no one else. If there was a purpose to life, Sanae was it. "What are you doing outside on a day like this?" she asked.

"Hi, Mom," Sanae said. "Masako and Natsumi and I were talking. We were going to play inside, but I think we'll go back to the school playground instead."

"I invited Yukari to come for dinner," Nozomi said.

"Well, we're going to the playground," Sanae said.

"Oh," Nozomi said, "can Yukari go too?"

Yukari looked at Sanae. Although her family lived virtually across the street, being younger than Sanae meant that they didn't play often. Yukari showed signs already, however, of worshipping Sanae the way her mother adored Nozomi.

"Sure she can," Sanae said.

"Be careful," Nozomi said and turned toward their home, a two story house with a small garden in front. There was a letter from the neighborhood association as well as a notice from Sanae's school in the mailbox. Less mail now since most of their bills were paid through the bank. Nozomi unlocked the translucent glass front door to slide it open. She moved inside and kicked off her boots, stepped up from the entryway and flicked on a light.

The house looked clean. It should, she thought, having cleaned in the morning. This morning, yesterday morning, the morning before. She went to the bathroom to heat the water for a bath. Nozomi turned the handle to put the gas flame on, but first checked under the plastic cover to see that there was actually water in it. One time she had turned the heat on when the bath was empty and almost set the house on fire. Another time she had melted the plastic replacement. Now the family had a metal bath.

There was a noise at the door. Most likely Hideki, her son. Recently he had grown so much. As if a new person had moved in with the family after all the years. It was unsettling how often he startled her.

"Door's open," she called. No one entered. "Just a minute."

Nozomi opened the door to find a nervous fifteen year-old girl. Although Nozomi was sure she didn't know her, the girl did look familiar. From one angle she bore a striking resemblance to Seiko Matsuda, possibly the country's most popular female singer. Perhaps that was it. Nozomi had just seen her on a television show presenting the week's most requested songs. The remarkable thing about this girl standing there was that she had already managed to copy exactly the hairstyle Seiko Matsuda had just introduced.

Another teenage girl stood back by the gate. The girl at the front door bowed. "Excuse me, Mrs. Matsuzaka," she said, "would you give this, please, to Hideki?" She handed Nozomi a light yellow envelope.

"He should be home soon," Nozomi said. "Would you like to wait inside?"

"Oh, no," the girl said. "Please excuse us."

"Please," Nozomi said, "I was so surprised. I thought it was Hideki."

The girls laughed. They were bobbing up and down now, bowing. "Excuse us."

They left. Nozomi stepped back inside. The situation was a first. Amusing. The girls were cute.

She put the letter down and turned on the television. She turned off the television. Why start now? There was another noise at the door.

"Mom," it was Sanae, "Yukari fell down. We stopped at her house, but her mother's not home yet." Sanae stood with her arm around Yukari who was covered with dirt and was crying, although she didn't seem to be hurt.

"Come in," Nozomi said. "Sanae, find some dry clothes for Yukari. What happened?"

They kicked off their shoes and Sanae ran upstairs. Masako explained that Yukari slipped on some ice on the way to the playground. Natsumi held Yukari's hand.

Sanae came down with a faded red jumpsuit. Masako began to arrange the shoes now, four tiny pairs of boots, so they would all face outward toward the door.

They moved to the back of the house. Nozomi pulled at Yukari's socks, but before long Sanae and Masako took over while Natsumi folded the clothing. Nozomi stood up.

"Thanks, Mom," Sanae said.

From the kitchen Nozomi heard the girls' voices gradually come back to normal. Then the sound of water. Nozomi decided to peel apples. She was sorry Sanae would grow up. She liked her exactly like this.

Nozomi's son Hideki came home next. "What's that on your shoulder?" she asked.

Hideki unslung a long canvas bag. "Coach asked me to take a few swings today," he said. "I have to practice."

"Coach?" Nozomi asked.

"Coach Shimazaki," Hideki said. "Baseball." He blew past his mother into the kitchen.

Other adults seemed to give the orders pretty easily these days. "You've never played baseball," she said.

"That's what *I* said," Hideki answered.

"And?"

"Coach said it didn't matter—because of my height." Hideki took a slight jump and put his palm on the kitchen ceiling.

Nozomi had never heard of such a thing. The baseball team was made up of players who started in little league and then continued through. "What about your studies at *juku?* We want to get into a good university, yes?" Hideki attended school after regular school from six until ten-thirty, five nights a week. "How can you go to *juku* and play baseball too?"

"Coach said he understood," Hideki answered.

"What does that mean?"

"The team needs some new players. He asked Hiroshi and me to try out." Being the tallest members of their class, the two were inseparable. "Don't worry, Mom. Nothing's been decided." He flexed his arm.

"I'm worried."

The girls emerged from the bathroom. Although they would have been interested in an older brother in any case, Hideki's height and good looks only added to their fascination. Since the sixth grade, Hideki had been taller than anyone on either side of the family.

Hideki noticed Yukari's jumpsuit. "Isn't that Sanae's?"

Yukari started to cry.

"What did I say?"

Hideki reached for the apples Nozomi had peeled.

"Those are for your sister and her friends."

"Sanae doesn't mind," Hideki said. He grabbed a handful of apple with one arm while pulling Sanae into a light headlock at the same time with his other. He took a bite of apple.

"Why do you do that?" Nozomi asked. She knew he wouldn't hurt his sister. He never had and he wouldn't. What was irritating was how much Sanae enjoyed it.

Hideki acted like he might grab Natsumi. Natsumi screamed and ran to Masako. Everybody seemed to be having a pretty good time except Nozomi and Yukari.

"What's for dinner?" Hideki asked. He let Sanae go so he could check the rice cooker.

"It's not ready," Nozomi said.

"I have to eat," Hideki said. "Do you want me to fall asleep in *juku* again?"

The girls laughed.

"I don't care where you fall asleep," Nozomi said.

"Come on, Mom," he said. "One minute you say that *juku* is the most important thing and now you don't care."

"Join the baseball team." Sports and girls, she knew, were the land mines. "See what kind of a university you get into."

Hideki took a rice bowl off the shelf.

"It's not ready," Nozomi repeated. "Have something else."

"I like it this way." He took a package of seaweed to sprinkle on the rice.

Nozomi offered the apples to the girls, but nobody wanted anything except to watch Hideki eat.

Nozomi remembered the yellow envelope. "You have a letter," she said.

"From who?"

"Two girls stopped by."

"Who?"

"Don't you know?" Nozomi asked.

"How could I know? Didn't you get their names?"

"No. But one of them looked a little bit like Seiko Matsuda."

"Oooh," the girls sighed. To look like Seiko Matsuda was an enviable fate.

Hideki turned bright red.

The girls giggled.

"Got to go," he said. *"Juku.* Hiroshi's waiting at the station."

"Don't you want to see the letter?"

"What letter?" He walked quickly from the house.

The phone rang. Toshio, most likely. Nozomi felt glad. Maybe he would come home early tonight. She wanted to speak with her husband.

Sanae answered. It was her grandmother, Nozomi's mother-in-law. A woman with an unerring instinct for the uncomfortable moment. A woman whose mission in life had grown into making the people around her miserable.

60

Especially her two daughters by marriage. Had they lived twenty, fifty or a hundred years before, the situation would have manifested itself as an unspoken struggle over territory—kitchen, closet, bedroom. Information and experience versus youth and beauty. A drama played through generation after generation of households, only now shaken loose by increasing affluence and mobility. Kiyomi Matsuzaka, Nozomi's mother-in-law, was not pleased about the changes.

"For you, Mom," Sanae said.

Nozomi picked up the phone. "Toshio?" her mother-in-law asked. Her specialty was to make people feel like they didn't exist.

"Toshio is at work," Nozomi said.

"Ask him to call me," she said. "Problems with the plumbing again."

"I understand," Nozomi said.

"Is everything all right?"

"Yes, Mother," Nozomi said.

"Something in your voice."

"Everything is all right."

"Good," she said. "Be well."

"You too," Nozomi replied. It was their third conversation of the day. Mrs. Matsuzaka had called twice earlier in the morning and spoken with Nozomi for twenty minutes and forty minutes. Nozomi categorized her mother-in-law's phone calls in three ways. There was a "Toshio-has-not-been-the-same-since-he-got-married" phone call, a "modern-mothers-do-not-know-how-to-raise-children" phone call, and a "problems-with-the-plumbing-again" phone call.

Mrs. Matsuzaka had not forgiven her second son Toshio for buying her and her husband a new home. Toshio's mistake was to have preempted the family order, upsetting his older brother Kazuo's prerogative to provide for their parents. At the same time he had removed the forced opportunity for Mrs. Matsuzaka to manage a household at the expense of a daughter-in-law.

"Is Grandma coming to live with us again?" Sanae asked. There had been one miserable period when Toshio's parents had moved in with them while Toshio had replaced their plumbing. Nozomi was not eager to repeat the experience.

"I don't think so."

"That's good," Sanae said. Natsumi and Masako laughed.

Nozomi did not want to encourage her. "I need some tofu," she said. Tofu she had forgotten earlier. "Can you get it for me?"

"Silk texture or cotton?" Sanae asked.

"Cotton would be fine," Nozomi said. "Afterwards, you'll have to do some homework." This was a cue for Natsumi and Masako.

"What about Yukari?" Sanae asked.

Yukari seemed anxious to reestablish her competence in life. "Yukari can go too," Nozomi said.

The girls left. Nozomi took some vegetables out of the refrigerator. Working before dinner invariably cleared her mind. When the time comes, she thought, I want to be a different kind of mother-in-law.

There was a noise at the front door.

"Beer delivery," a voice called.

"You can leave it . . ." she started to say, but he had already entered. "Okay," she said, "bring it here."

Nozomi didn't like deliveries. She had heard the stories. Unhappy housewives and deliverymen. One of the few groups who could come and go without arousing suspicion. Nozomi thought about her own deliveries: newspaper, beer. Certain bills were still dropped by the house. The repairmen. It was true she often felt an uneasiness. She didn't know why they stood around or what they wanted. Someone to talk to, a break from the day, a cup of coffee. But no one had ever been rude to her. And none of her friends was involved with a deliveryman. Most of them—the newspaper boy, for example—were too improbable to imagine.

"Any returns?" he asked.

"Oh," she said, "of course, right here."

He took the empty bottles.

Nozomi looked at the clock. It was already 6:30. "You work hard, don't you?" she said.

"Excuse me," he tipped his cap and left.

Nozomi sat down at the table. She wanted to speak with her mother. Why didn't her own mother call more often? A daughter was considered to become a member of her husband's family on marriage, but Nozomi felt that her own mother had taken this too literally. How many times had her mother cut short a telephone conversation with an excuse such as they were running up the bill? Those times Nozomi wanted to scream, "Don't worry about the money, Mother. Forget it!"

Nozomi would not deny the hardship her parents had lived through, the poverty, hunger even. As farmers, the war had left them with nothing. No way out, it seemed. Farm prices were too low then to earn a living. What money they had saved at the postal service was never returned. How could it be? The war had taken everything. "A few people get rich—a lot of people die," her father had said about war. "That's all you need to know."

In those circumstances her parents had masked their discouragement and named their baby "Hope." Nozomi means hope. They took a stand against poor prospects by asking for nothing, against long odds by working long hours. Nozomi considered her parents to be heroes. She was sorry they seemed unable to take more pleasure from their labors.

There was no answer on the phone. Perhaps just as well. What would she and her mother discuss? What had they ever discussed? From the beginning, "Nozomi has a mind of her own," her mother would say. Nozomi was left, a girl in the country, to grow up alone.

Those days she took walks along the river. She watched the trains and the fishermen, the construction workers and the cars. She studied the changes in the colors and the birds above, wondering about other places, newer places. Places where no one said you should, you must or you have to.

As a girl Nozomi knew the train schedule by heart. To Tokyo. From Tokyo. But every time she looked it seemed that the train was headed for Tokyo.

Sanae returned with Yukari. "The lady at the tofu store gave us scallions for the tofu," Sanae said.

"Did she?"

"Yes," Yukari grinned, "and she said to put it with ginger and soy sauce."

"Did you say thank you?" Nozomi asked.

The girls nodded.

"Well, then," Nozomi said, "let's eat."

Sanae did not have to ask about her father. Dinner at home had become the exception. His business was active. He was needed elsewhere. Nozomi was not always happy about it, but she understood. Toshio had his responsibilities, she had hers.

The three ate quietly. After dinner Sanae went upstairs to do her homework. Nozomi cleaned the kitchen and started with Yukari's clothing. Yukari watched television.

When Nozomi finished washing she sat down with Yukari in front of the television. Cartoons were ending. News would follow. After that a documentary, "Japan: Thirty-Five Years of Economic Miracle." Nozomi usually liked documentaries, but this one was nothing new.

64

About nine o'clock, Akiko stopped by to pick up Yukari. She brought tangerines. "They were on sale," she said. "I bought too many." She looked at Yukari. "What happened to your dress?"

"I fell," Yukari explained.

Nozomi apologized to Akiko.

"No," Akiko said, "I should be the one to apologize."

"Anyway," Nozomi said, "the important thing is that Yukari is all right. I'll bring her clothes over tomorrow when they've dried."

"Don't think of it," Akiko said. "I'll come get them."

Nozomi smiled. It was kinder to let Akiko resolve the situation. "Fine," she said. "By the way, who's watching your baby?"

"Masaaki," Akiko replied.

"Masaaki?" Nozomi asked. Masaaki was Akiko's husband, a jeweler. "Home already?"

"You know how Masaaki is," Akiko said. "He doesn't like to go out at night."

Nozomi nodded. Masaaki was fourteen years older than Akiko. Their marriage had been arranged. Nozomi had worried when Akiko married—what did Akiko know about men? That it had worked out so well surprised Nozomi.

"Masaaki," Akiko repeated.

"Mom," Sanae appeared at the top of the stairs, "I'm going to sleep now."

"We're leaving," Akiko said. "Yukari should go to sleep too."

"Sanae," Nozomi said, "come down and say good-bye."

"I'll stop by tomorrow," Akiko said and then she thanked Nozomi five or six times before leaving.

Nozomi and Sanae went upstairs. It was Nozomi's favorite time of day, just the two of them. Maybe they couldn't talk about so many things yet. It didn't matter.

Nozomi liked the feeling they had. Sometimes Sanae would fall asleep while Nozomi sat in her room.

The house was quiet, a little cold. After years in the same house Nozomi was still experimenting with the right combination of gas heaters and stand-up kerosene stoves. Gas, she knew, was not completely safe because leaks were possible. Fumes from kerosene stoves were worse and required an open window. Electricity was no help. Electric heaters were extremely expensive to use and didn't throw off much heat.

There always seemed to be a chill in the house somewhere. Even in the heated rooms, even if the stoves were lit and the right doors were closed, somehow, from somewhere, a cold draft would slip in. The only way really to get warm was to take a bath. That was always good for a couple hours' warmth. Nozomi usually took hers between the time Sanae went to sleep and the time Hideki came home.

Nozomi placed the yellow envelope the two girls had brought earlier on Hideki's desk. She was relieved it was well-sealed because she knew she would have been tempted to read it.

Hideki came home just before eleven, a different character after *juku*. Nozomi always prepared a tray of food for him, but tonight, exhausted, he just took a bath and went to sleep. To see him so tired reminded Nozomi he was still a boy.

When Hideki went to sleep Nozomi was never really sure what to do. Toshio could come home any minute or he might not come home until later, perhaps as late as two-thirty or three. A phone call was rare; when she asked him to call, he said to expect him late. Furthermore, she never knew if he would come home drunk or sober, whether he would want to eat or would have eaten, whether he would want to have sex or wouldn't, or would want to have sex and be unable.

That had happened too. There was no way to anticipate. Each night from eleven or so she waited.

Sometimes Reiko called, a phone call that didn't help. Katsuichiro, her husband, was a well-placed manager with a large trading company and was obligated to lots of entertainment with clients and office colleagues. Each year, they agreed, the situation grew worse—later and later, drunker and more indifferent on arrival.

The kitchen felt cold. Winter was cold. Nozomi pushed up the heat and took a magazine from her stack on the table. "Tokyo, Eastern Capital," the cover read. The article traced Tokyo's development from the Edo period when political control was moved to the present metropolis with the most cash, most policemen, most vending machines, most bars, most commuters, et cetera. It was hard to maintain interest and Nozomi was tired. You live in Tokyo, she told herself.

She put the magazine down and turned on the television. She wasn't proud of it, but occasionally she watched "Eleven PM," a program that looked for any excuse to talk about sex or present a mostly naked body. There were girls from clubs, girls from resorts, girls from who knows where. A little conversation, another body. Nozomi couldn't say she was truly interested in this. She was bored. At this particular moment, she was cold too.

Thirty-five years of economic miracle, she thought, and I'm freezing.

FOUR

Even doing so little the days passed too quickly.

Nozomi fought the feeling that her children did not need her as they once had needed her. She'd caught snippets of Sanae and her friends talking about boys recently. It was happening too soon.

Nozomi went into the bedroom and kneeled in front of her mirror. She was still a good-looking woman, she thought, but she was not looking good. She heard a joke recently. "Japanese women are like Christmas cakes. After the twenty-fifth, nobody wants them." Nozomi knew the feeling. A feeling of having been used and done with.

The phone rang. Akiko. Nozomi laughed at herself. Akiko had been satisfied to marry on little more than two meetings and the understanding that by coincidence she would be moving into Nozomi's neighborhood.

"Nozomi," she asked, "a bad time?"

"No," Nozomi said, "but a little busy."

"I'd rather talk when you have time."

"Thank you." Nozomi hung up.

Music came blaring from the neighbors. Why did they let that girl listen to music all the time? She didn't go to school

68

and she didn't work or if she did, it was just odd hours. Nozomi tried to make out who was singing. At least the girl did have one talent. Next week's most popular song was already playing on her record player this week. Nozomi had always disapproved of the way her parents had raised her.

Nozomi did not know what she was thinking about these days. Only that she was haunted by a continuing and growing feeling that somewhere along the way she had made a mistake (a mistake she could not isolate), missed an opportunity, lost a chance.

She decided to fry some noodles. There was time before Sanae would be home. She could eat and be cleaned up by then. She put a small piece of lard into a pan, turned on the flame and took out some vegetables. Just cutting the vegetables helped set her mind in order. Room by room she began to organize herself. Clothing, food, finances, the house. School, the car. Had she put the children's clothes away? She couldn't remember. Strange. How did the bathroom look? Should she clean it? Nozomi turned the flame down to take a quick look around the house. The clothes weren't put away. That only took a second. She checked the bathroom. What a mess that was. She started to straighten up. It didn't take long, but what a smell! Was this her bathroom? Oh, my God, she thought. The lard was burning. She would have to air the house.

Take the afternoon off. Once she cleared her mind, it would be easy to get the house in order, or at least on the road to order. On impulse she decided to look at her kimonos. Upstairs she opened the chest made specially to hold them. Most she received for her wedding. They still fit, but she had probably looked at them more times than she had worn them. What it must have put her parents through to give her this set of kimonos—kimonos for weddings, festivals, funerals. But how glad she was to have them.

Even unworn, lying there as they were. The colors they bore: yellows and brown, deep reds and blues. The work that had gone into them. Even when she wasn't wearing them—even unheld in the sureness of their wrap—she could feel their guiding hand. The certainty, steadiness, reliability, tradition. The generation after generation of women through whose experience they flowed.

Nozomi closed the drawer and went downstairs. She would play the videotape of Akiko's younger sister's wedding. Of course this is what Akiko had called about. Nozomi had had the tape for almost a week and hadn't played it. She could have been invited to the wedding, but because she didn't really know Akiko's sister she had declined. She had not wanted to be one of the few non-family women at the reception, she hadn't felt like committing to the trip, and she felt foolish asking Toshio to go when she knew he wouldn't want to. "Will they videotape it?" Nozomi had asked.

"Of course."

"Please excuse us then. You know how Toshio is about weddings."

Akiko knew. Toshio did not like them. Least of all with Nozomi. Something too painful about the hopefulness on the faces of the newlyweds.

Nozomi put the videotape on. It was a Christian ceremony. Akiko's sister wore a white wedding dress.

Music came blasting again from the girl's stereo next door. Nozomi knew the themes all too well. First kisses, holding hands, boyfriends, misunderstandings, reconciliations, marriage, honeymoons. Akiko's sister and her husband had gone to Hawaii. Probably on a honeymoon tour with five or six other couples.

Sanae walked in with her friends Natsumi and Masako. Instinctively they moved to the television and sat intently before the picture. Nozomi had an uneasy feeling about seeing what had already become these girls' ultimate, all-encompassing goal: marriage. "Could we start it from the beginning?" Sanae asked.

Why not? She hadn't been watching long. Nozomi rewound the tape and the four watched together. Occasionally one of the girls asked a question about procedure or detail. Usually one of the other girls answered. Sometimes they would make a comment as to how appropriate one of the songs was—all Western pop songs— or how beautiful one of the three wedding gowns looked. There was a white Western wedding dress, then a traditional kimono, then a Western-style evening gown. After the meal, the men and the sister's best friend offered toasts of congratulations. The tape featured each table at some point to show the guests. Nozomi was surprised to spot a short take of Akiko and her mother standing behind one of the tables being featured; unmistakably they were having some kind of argument.

Short, bald and nearsighted Masaaki, Akiko's husband, spoke warmly and humorously after stumbling at first with some stuttered words and a microphone screech. Nozomi felt that she had underestimated him.

At the end of the tape the girls wanted to watch again. Nozomi had some things to prepare for dinner and said that she thought the girls had better things to do, but if they really wanted to watch again she would let them.

Nozomi stepped into the kitchen. Rather than starting right away she picked up a magazine. She felt nervous. Where was Hideki? He hadn't called. *Juku* would start soon.

Nozomi closed the magazine and walked out to the living room to watch the videotape once more. Already on second viewing, the girls were able to recall key parts of speeches, including slips, from memory. When they finished watching again Sanae asked Nozomi to tell them what marriage was really like. Sanae asked with utmost sincerity, revealing how closely she already held this institution to her personal destiny. Alone Nozomi might have joked with her, but the presence of the other girls recommended a different tack.

Marriage depends on the man, she wanted to say.

"Marriage is serious," she said. The girls nodded.

"Isn't that true," Natsumi said.

"I really think it is," Masako said.

The girls wanted to watch a third time.

The phone rang. "Hideki," he said. "Can't talk, Mom. Late for *juku*. Hiroshi ran into some trouble. Had to help."

He sounded like a telegraph operator. "What kind of trouble?" she asked.

"Don't worry," he said. "Everything's all right now."

"Why didn't you call earlier?" Nozomi thought she heard some giggling in the background.

"I didn't have change," he said.

"Don't tell your mother you didn't have change."

"I'm sorry. Mom, listen. *Juku* starts in two minutes. I have to go." He paused. "Okay?"

She knew why he hadn't called earlier. It might interfere with his plans.

He hung up. Hideki had learned from his father.

Nozomi returned to the kitchen and picked up the magazine again, *Break*. Photojournalism at its most popular, two pages of picture and text related to each topic—gossip, the unusual and the absurd preferred. She hadn't often read *Break*, but she liked it recently when Toshio brought it home. She turned to an article on group sex and started reading, but it was hard to concentrate. To be touched, she thought, well, at least in a certain way.

Toshio appeared in the doorway.

"You," she said.

"Yes."

"You're home."

"That's right," he said. "What are you reading?"

"*Break*." She wanted to bury it. She closed the magazine and handed it to Toshio.

"I think we have some ads in this issue." He turned to the article on group sex and opened it for Nozomi's benefit. The picture showed the backs of five or six middle-aged bodies.

"I'd like to try it," he said. "Any interest?"

"Don't be an idiot," she said.

"Group sex," he said. "You and me."

She laughed.

"Daddy," Sanae came running in, "what's wrong? You're home so early."

"Nothing's wrong," he said.

Nozomi did not like the way Sanae was looking at her father. It didn't seem fair. Nozomi had spent all the time with the children. She should have a closer hold on their affections.

"I got a surprise call at the office today," Toshio said, "a Coach Shimazaki. He said he was the new baseball coach at the high school. He said he wanted to talk about Hideki. I thought it was some kind of joke. Why should Ryo Shimazaki call me? For a second I even thought . . .with all the kooks around . . ."

He didn't have to say it. Nozomi knew. The world was growing more and more dangerous all the time.

"Who would believe that Ryo Shimazaki was calling me?" Toshio laughed. "I almost declared an office holiday."

Ryo Shimazaki had secured a place for himself as a minor legend in Japanese baseball lore. A thin man who had traced out a spotty career as a pinch hitter and utility infielder for the Yakumi Bears, Shimazaki had succeeded on little more than determination, a story that began when he failed to make the cut for his high school baseball team. Instead of quitting like so many would have, he volunteered to help with the equipment. From that position he climbed all the way to the majors. Fans had loved him. "Ryo! Ryo! Ryo!" they cheered. During his four years in the majors Ryo exemplified the power of will. He would do anything for his team. In one unforgettable incident, Ryo threw himself in front of a pitch in order to be hit by the ball—collect first base and force in the winning run. The umpires conferred for several minutes in an effort to find a consensus as to the legality of Shimazaki's play. Perhaps there really was no choice. Shimazaki was called safe and awarded first base. As the head umpire was quoted later on the nationally televised sports round-up, "I wouldn't recommend it," he said, "but we felt we could not interpret the rules." All over the country, little leaguers who could not hit began to throw themselves in front of pitches. Major league baseball had to amend its rules. Ryo appeared on national television to plead with younger players to protect themselves, to try and hit. Baseball changed its rules because of Ryo!

"He said he'd been named coach at Hideki's high school," Toshio said. "I couldn't believe it."

Retired from active participation as a player himself, Ryo had taken the head coaching job at his high school alma mater in Yokohama and developed its program into one of the nation's finest. Over the last twelve or fifteen years, Ryo's teams could often be seen chalking up big wins in the nationally televised spring and fall baseball tournaments. Shimazaki had become a synonym for success, Shimazaki itself being transformed into a verb: "to shimazaki" an opponent meant to win by ten or more runs.

Only about a year before, however, after perhaps a few beers too many, Ryo swore on the "National Sports Round-Up" that his team was so good that year that if it didn't

74

deliver the national fall tournament he would find the worst high school baseball team in the country and stick with the team until it became a winner. Ryo's team did not make it, losing a 2-1 decision in the final game. In sports papers across the country, "to shimazaki" began to take on other meanings as well.

Following the season Ryo spent three weeks in a Zen retreat in humility and meditation so as to contemplate his future. Certainly there was a part of himself that wanted to dismiss the statement he had made on television as words spoken in the heat of battle, and to accept the forgiveness and countenance offered by school officials who were in truth overjoyed at Ryo's performance, the spirit of his players, Ryo's generally impeccable character, and the ever increasing ticket sales.

Ryo retired to the mountain for those three weeks and discovered what he had perhaps known all along. To retain his integrity he would need to follow the dictates of his previously spoken words. Thus he moved quickly and arranged to take the position of head baseball coach at Hideki's high school, a school hardly known for athletics, but known instead for its academics and . . . for its girls.

"He said that he wants to meet me tonight," Toshio said. "At first I assumed he wanted help in putting out a call for support among the parents. He said it was simpler. He wants to talk about Hideki joining the team."

"Why didn't you call me earlier?" Nozomi reacted.

"Maybe you had made plans," he said. "I didn't want to obligate you."

"What kind of plans?" Nozomi asked. "My obligations are here." At least there was one sense of relief. She knew why Hideki had not come home from school. "Did you say anything else?"

"Of course I did," Toshio answered. "I told him about Hideki's commitment to *juku*, that he was college-bound. I told him that Hideki had never played baseball before and that I didn't understand how he could possibly participate in an organized program at this point."

"What did he say?"

"He said he would have never approached Hideki, but that Hideki had approached him. He said that Hideki had begged for a tryout."

It was hard to believe. "What time is he coming?" Nozomi asked.

"I have to confirm. If you'd rather we can go out."

"He's welcome at seven-thirty," she said. "I wouldn't dream of your going out."

"Thank you," Toshio said.

"Sanae," Nozomi was moving, "your room needs straightening. You can take a look at your brother's room too, please." There might not be a chance in the world Coach Shimazaki would see anything other than the living room and the urinal in the downstairs bathroom, but Nozomi was not taking any chances. She would take care of the more public areas herself. Sanae could help behind the scenes.

Natsumi and Masako went home reluctantly.

Toshio made the call to Shimazaki who arrived promptly at 7:30 with a younger man whom he introduced as his assistant coach. Shimazaki carried a small gift, which he gave to Nozomi. That such a man had become a sports legend was surprising. He was shorter than she was, pigeon-toed and except for monstrous calves, which she noticed when he was taking off his shoes, there was nothing about him that said athlete. His assistant on the other hand, looked much more like an athlete. Nozomi guessed that he was in his late twenties, but somehow, she sensed, he was frozen at a developmental level that roughly approximated high school baseball. He was excessively polite—bowing, nodding and averting his eyes. Nozomi knew to be cautious around people who were polite that way. In the end, she had learned too many times that people who are polite with no sense of themselves can be rudest of all.

Nozomi seated the men and asked if they would care for a beer. In spite of Toshio's urging, Shimazaki insisted that tea would be fine. Nozomi went into the kitchen to heat water, but checked in any case to make sure the refrigerator was well-stocked. This monkish pretense would not last long, she knew. She put a couple of extra bottles into the freezer to be ready. While the water was heating she opened the present Shimazaki had brought. Imported chocolate. Nozomi brought the tea out and poured. She would have liked to stay, but her small talk did not feel natural and seemed to make Toshio uncomfortable. She asked if they wanted something to eat before retreating to the kitchen. The coaches said that they had eaten dinner already. Nozomi confirmed her supplies nonetheless. The ricemaker was full. She might need it.

The phone rang. Reiko. Nozomi did not feel like talking, but Reiko needed a more complete explanation than Akiko had. "Toshio is entertaining a new baseball coach named Ryo Shimazaki."

"You're kidding?" Reiko said. "Ryo Shimazaki?"

"I'm not kidding," Nozomi said. "Why?"

"I saw him on television this morning," Reiko said. "I'm coming over."

"Wait," Nozomi said abruptly. "The men are talking."

"Well," Reiko seemed defensive, "some exciting news on this end too."

"Yes?"

"The cafe bar," she said, "a possible location."

"That's great, Reiko."

"Isn't it? Let's talk when you're less busy."

"Thank you, Reiko."

"*Ciao*," Reiko liked to use foreign words when she was feeling good.

"*Oi!*" Toshio called from the living room. "Nozomi! Something to eat!"

"Coming," she said. The tray was prepared.

"These, Mom?" Sanae asked.

"Thank you." Sanae took the beers out of the freezer and began to open them.

"Bring us some beers," Toshio yelled.

"Yes," Nozomi said, "coming." She slid the door open to carry the food and drink out to the living room. The men sat cross-legged around a short table with a heater attached underneath in the middle. For Toshio sitting cross-legged was actually somewhat awkward, having never completely mastered the position. He had trouble keeping his right leg down.

"You have a fine, healthy son," Shimazaki said to Nozomi.

"Thank you," Nozomi said.

"A fine young man, and perhaps a natural athlete. Did you play sports?" he asked Toshio.

"No."

"Where does he get it?" he asked.

"You should see the way he eats," Toshio said. "Meat, bread, potatoes. The only thing he likes is American food."

"That's funny," Shimazaki said. "I'm told they're eating rice now in America."

"Nothing would surprise me anymore," Toshio said. "My son is fifteen and he can't use chopsticks."

The coaches began to fill their plates. "This food is delicious," the assistant coach said before he tasted it.

When Nozomi left the room, Toshio mused that this could be a good forum in which to present a baseball strategy he had worked out years ago, but never had a good opportunity to discuss. Nozomi could tell that Shimazaki must have really wanted Hideki because of the way he listened to Toshio's idea. Toshio said that he always wondered why in a situation with no men on base and with no strikes or with one strike on the batter (before the catcher has to worry about catching the ball to earn the strike-out), why didn't managers ever pull the catcher to use somewhere else in the field? Was there a rule about this? The coaches didn't think so. Did a pitcher need a catcher to perform well?

Shimazaki looked at Toshio, lifted his plate and placed a generous portion of food into his mouth.

"Especially against the bunt," Toshio said. "You could have the man practically standing on top of the plate."

"Perhaps," Shimazaki said as a concession that he had never considered Toshio's unusual strategy.

The men drank heavily while the conversation turned more serious. Nozomi could hear bits and pieces from the kitchen when she was bringing out more food or beer. Shimazaki railed against all the press and attention that had been focused on Japan's success being due to imitation— that Japan had succeeded as a society because it borrowed from other cultures. Toshio did not know why Shimazaki was worrying about this, but he did know that he shared surprisingly strong feelings on the matter.

"There is an original Japanese culture," Shimazaki said. "Consider the uniqueness of our cuisine."

Nozomi laughed to herself. It was funny to hear a baseball coach using words like cuisine. She knew she was losing the battle.

"And what about music?" Shimazaki continued. "What about our three metered music? There's no music like that in Korea. Where did that come from?"

Toshio and the assistant coach looked at each other. "China?" the assistant coach asked.

"No, not China," Shimazaki said. "Not China. It had to have been developed here."

"Isn't that something," Toshio responded.

"There are clues to this puzzle if you know how to look," Shimazaki said, "but you have to know how to look."

"Interesting," Toshio said. "I'll have to spend more time thinking about these things." He took a deep breath. "Nozomi! Coffee!"

Nozomi took out the coffee beans she had purchased to be ready for such an occasion. To her frustration the machine was not working. Toshio came in, but he couldn't get the machine to work either. "Make it instant," he said. The door to the living room was open. "You've got this machine so messed up nobody can use it."

Nozomi cleared the plates and empty bottles. For a moment she felt a sharp, directed anger about her treatment, the lack of courtesy and grace from Toshio, in particular, and from men in general. She had an impulse to act selfishly herself. Why not? This business of silently bearing things, what was it worth?

She started to wash the dishes. Perhaps it was better not to worry so much, she thought. Toshio's behavior was natural. Did she really want women to act like men? What would things be like then?

The coaches finished their coffee and departed.

Nozomi heated some water for tea. Toshio decided he would have tea too, even after a cup and a half of coffee. They sat in silence. Hideki arrived about ten minutes after the coaches had left, as if on cue. Wisely, he chose to make a brief appearance, polite and deferential. "Everything is okay," he said, adding that he'd had dinner and that in the future he would try to come home between school and *juku*. He asked to be excused. Nozomi did not feel like pressing.

"Good night," Toshio said.

After a period of silence, Nozomi eventually said, "He's going to need a new calculator soon—with a memory."

"I have one at the office," Toshio said. "I'll bring it home tomorrow."

"He can't take your calculator to *juku?*" Nozomi said.

"Why not?"

"Because everyone else will have new ones."

They lapsed into silence again until Toshio began to expound on how *juku* had become too concerned with memorization. "Repetition may be helpful toward passing the exams," he said, "but what about character? How can you develop if you're in a classroom all day? You should have heard some of the things Shimazaki said."

"The point is that those exams mean a good university and a good university means a successful career."

"Do you think I'm going to give the office to someone else's son because Hideki didn't go to a good enough university?" Toshio asked. "He goes to a good high school now. Why not take a break from *juku* for a year or two? Maybe he wants to do other things."

"It's hard to start up again once you take a break," she said. "Besides, he'll need skills to run the agency. To be successful."

"Ryo Shimazaki." Toshio said. "Nozomi, I have to thank you."

"Toshio!"

"Nozomi, do you know what it takes to make it in advertising?"

"No."

81

"Not much," he laughed. "Why not let the boy have some fun?"

Nozomi went upstairs to check on Sanae. Toshio could either fall asleep in the living room or he could follow her up. The sight of Sanae sleeping revived Nozomi's spirits. Toshio straggled up the stairs. "Isn't she beautiful?" Nozomi asked and held the door open so Toshio could see.

"She's beautiful," he said, marching past. "Big day today," he said on his way to the bedroom. "Nothing's been decided," he continued to himself. "We'll jump off that bridge when we come to it."

Nozomi joined him in the bedroom. Perhaps things had not turned out exactly as she had hoped. The choices would be different for Sanae.

"Ryo Shimazaki in our house," Toshio said as Nozomi crawled into bed.

"I'm glad you're happy," she said.

Toshio rolled closer, put his head on her shoulder. He felt comfortable, happy. She was his wife. He let his hand roam south. She was wet. He hoisted a leg, but she felt so muscular, tense. "Do you want me to stop?" he asked.

She shook her head no.

"Why don't you say something then?"

"I'm concentrating on what we're doing," she said.

What did that mean? Toshio started again. The problem was that they had no lift-off anymore. It was easier to think about other women. He thought about Yuko, his model. Yuko had been to the office twice now. She was, thanks to his assistance, going to land the assignment. He liked her, the way she looked, the way she acted. The short skirts she wore and her stockings underneath. I try to get a picture in my mind, he imagined himself telling her. Starting with her skirt. I try to get a picture in my mind, he thought. Her stockings now. He could touch her. Get to her panties, he thought. Coming was hard. He was pulling her stockings down, but she wouldn't kiss him.

—Always Nozomi liked the way that gloves felt. And stockings. And that when she was working she could buy stockings right in the store. And gloves. And that she could afford stockings and gloves because she was working, and managed her money well. And that she could wear stockings and gloves when she met him. And he was nervous. But she was nervous. And he cared. But she cared. They took walks together. Then more and more walks. He proposed. She had hoped for this. She was happy. She felt warm inside.

Toshio felt weakened. After sex it was woman's constancy, not his own. He felt like something had been taken from him. "Nothing to say?" he asked.

"Did you lock the door downstairs?"

Women change when they get married, he thought.

Nozomi lay steadfastly. The choices would be different for Sanae, she thought. Or would they?

Toshio felt angry on his way to the office. He had slept badly and dreamt that he'd awakened on the Korean side of town. Too often at home lately he'd had the feeling of being in the wrong place. He would stay away, farther away. He was busy. It was allowable.

On his desk was a proposal to improve the image of one of the smaller chemical companies. Small was a relative word, this company being enormous by almost any other standard. Toshio was pleased when Diamond Advertising had been invited to bid for the job and could see that it represented a possible ticket to bigger things. The company had had difficulties recently because of health problems its effluents had caused in communities neighboring its plants. Diamond Advertising was proposing no less than a high-visibility national advertising offensive to overcome these difficulties. Toshio had been pleased with Tahara's suggestion for the theme: "Building Better Lives," but when the group had begun to backpedal about the credibility of such an approach, Toshio had been forced to deliver his "Everyone who goes to the beauty parlor will not come out beautiful" speech. Toshio saved it for special occasions, but had felt the need more and more often lately as the idealism of several of his younger salarymen began occasionally to interfere with their ability to see things realistically.

Toshio put the presentation down and picked up a summary report prepared by his accountant. He was surprised he had missed it before; sitting right on his desk like that, surely he would have looked at it first. Toshio paged through his financial situation. The word "swimmingly," came to mind. Not great, but no real problems, either. A little elbow room at last. He had stopped wasting time having to shift funds or deplete accounts. Besides the firm, which he owned by himself, he had a good-sized equity in the two homes, three small bank accounts where he kept a little cash salted away, a few odds and ends in his stock portfolio—not much, but there—and a little gambling money in his commodity account. Funny, even with the money in it, the commodity account felt more like a liability than an asset. He wondered whether Nozomi had been putting money aside over the years from the household funds. He assumed so; she was entitled.

Toshio knew that Diamond Advertising would not get the chemical account. His firm had done a good job, but a small-time job—not enough research, not enough thinking. He wondered if Diamond Advertising had been included to set things up for one of the larger firms. Maybe. He would have to hire better in the future. He could take advantage of his financial stability to broaden his base. It was worth the investment. If things held together for another five or eight

84

years he would have his piece of the pie. Growing with the country. That was the key. Growing with the country. He wondered if his brother in the Foreign Ministry would be the one to cause the country's downfall, embarrassing the nation and spiting his younger brother.

A telephone call interrupted his reverie.

"Do you know who this is?" a young girl's voice asked.

"Of course," he said, not knowing. How could he know? She started talking before he knew who she was.

"Who?" she asked.

"Line what?" Toshio said as if talking to somebody else. "Just a second, excuse me," he said and put her on hold. He worked the voice over in his mind, but couldn't place it.

"Mitsue . . ." he said over the intercom.

"Yuko Tanioka," she answered. The new model.

Toshio was surprised. He had just been thinking about her. Talking on the phone was different. "Thank you, Mitsue," he said. At least Mitsue had had the presence of mind to put the girl through. He wondered at what point he would have to ask her not to.

"Sorry to keep you holding, Yuko," he said. "How are you?"

"I'm fine," she said. "I called to thank you for helping me get the job."

"I didn't help you," he said. "You earned it." He could feel himself growing flush, afraid to think this could really be happening.

"Thanks to you," she said and giggled.

If you feel it, it's there, he thought. "When do we shoot?" he asked.

"Soon," she said. "Don't you know?"

Of course he knew. "Well, not exactly," he said. "We're a little busy around here, working." Toshio thought about their interview. She was tall, young and had seemed to be a bit uncoordinated, he could sense this even as she was sitting there—this was his first impression. She was not beautiful, but she was cute. And cute was all right. In fact, cute was good. She'd shown a different look both times he had seen her. Also good for a model. And besides all this she had another quality Toshio would have liked to, but could not quite put his finger on. Certainly not sophistication. As a model, she clearly had some things to learn. "Have you done much modeling before?" he asked.

"No," she said. They laughed.

He liked her. There was a silence. Toshio was afraid to say anything. It was still business, right? The last thing the agency needed was for her to mess up the shoot. "Yuko," he said, "we hope the job goes well and we hope you'll be able to do a lot of things with us down the line. Call me anytime." Had he gone too far? Toshio felt the spine-chilling possibility that this wasn't Yuko after all. What if it was on behalf of Nozomi? One of Nozomi's friends? "What?" Toshio asked.

"I didn't say anything," she said. The conversation stumbled to an end.

Toshio felt alternately excited that Yuko had called and also annoyed with himself that he hadn't been more effective. He'd been nervous. He had to be careful. She might be setting him up. But let her set him up. What was there to hide? He wanted to be set up. He would show her. He imagined himself taking her into his office. "Here," he would say, "like this." He wondered if she still lived with her parents.

Something new had begun, he thought, not sure just what. He hoped he would be able to deal with her. Nowadays with girls it seemed as if it all came down to either love or money. Toshio liked a little in between.

Shibata barged into the office. A salaryman, to use the word loosely. Looking at the crumpled figure in front of him, Toshio tried to remember the last time Shibata had had a good idea.

Toshio conducted the meeting with his mind on Yuko. Maybe he hadn't done so badly. She would call again; if not, he could always reach her. They were forced to have contact. Uncertainty was part of the package, part of the excitement. Beginnings were even the best part—before the inevitable social contract set in and things began to lose their spirit.

Shibata was saying something about a party for Diamond Advertising's clients in June.

"In June?" Toshio asked. "Why are we worrying about that now?"

"We're not worrying," Shibata said. "We discussed it at the meeting yesterday . . ." Shibata's words receded into the walls.

It was more satisfying to think about Yuko. Yuko-*chan*. Toshio addressed her more affectionately now as he would a child or a daughter. From this angle, like this, he imagined himself saying to her.

Shibata was looking at Toshio.

"Okay, okay," Toshio said. "It sounds like a good idea. Tell Mitsue to pencil it down in my appointment book." We can erase it later, he thought.

Shibata nodded and walked from the office.

Toshio looked at the papers on his desk. Too much mail, too many messages. Keeping up, always keeping up. That was the key. Success itself inseparable from one's role in the machine. Affluence or the possibility of such, the blessing of having lived in a certain place and time. Business conditions were good, the country was at peace. The pie had grown bigger and a share was worth that much more.

)

"I'm sorry," Mitsue said over the intercom, "I have three people on the line at once. Shun Ozaki, your mother and your wife. What shall I tell them?"

You can tell them Coach Ryo Shimazaki says there is an original Japanese culture if you know how to look, he imagined saying, *then put them all through on a party line.*

As for himself there was only one proof needed to establish the country's independent evolution. No thinking people, he understood, would have ever copied the overbearing social structure they now called their own. It had to have been developed internally.

FIVE

Toshio looked at his calendar. It felt more like June—rainy season—humid and muggy, uncomfortable. Days that reminded Toshio of how he felt when he had the flu. But where was spring? Between winter's cold, summer's discomfort, the awful humidity of the rainy season and the inconvenience of the typhoon season, wasn't the country entitled to a little nice weather?

Tahara came in.

"Tahara," Toshio said, "call our landlord and see what we can do about some air conditioning."

"We called," Tahara said. "He said that if the building converts to air conditioning we'll lose the heat for the rest of the year. He said that it's still too early to do that." A bead of perspiration rolled down his forehead.

"I think we could sacrifice the heat," Toshio said. "Don't you?"

Tahara nodded.

Mitsue buzzed. "Hiroto Itoh," she said.

"Sit down," Toshio said to Tahara. "My new speaker phone. Digital. It compensates no matter how you throw out your voice."

89

"Moshi, moshi," Itoh said.

"Moshi, moshi," Toshio whispered. He winked at Tahara.

"What's wrong with your phone?" Itoh asked. "You sound like you're shouting in a tunnel."

"How are you?" Toshio asked.

"How are you?" Itoh answered emphatically.

"Everything's fine here," Toshio answered. "Did you paint the trucks?"

Itoh ignored Toshio's question. "We heard the news," he said, "about Big Catch Sushi." Word was leaking out, an embarrassment to the firm. "We want you to know that we're with you. We think that you're doing a terrific job for us and we're sure you'll be able to iron out everything in this other situation."

What was to iron out? They had canceled the ads. The only problem now was that everyone had to touch it. Everyone had to discuss it or get their two cents in.

"Government regulation," Itoh said, "is killing us."

"I appreciate the call," Toshio said. "Any response to the new color theme?"

"I'm not calling for myself," Itoh said, "but strictly to let you know that we're with you."

"That's nice to know," Toshio said, "believe me."

"Advertising is a dirty business," Itoh said.

It felt surprisingly good to hear this from a man who had made his fortune cleaning septic tanks. "Thank you," Toshio said.

"Any developments with Aoki Chemical?"

This was unexpected. "How do you know about Aoki Chemical?" Toshio asked.

"How do I know about Aoki Chemical?" Itoh asked. "We use the same bank. I'd like to see you get that account, Matsuzaka."

Why? Toshio wondered.

"Life is not a one-way street. We have to stick together."

"Thank you."

"Don't thank me," Itoh said. "I know you would do the same."

"I would do the same," Toshio said. Unfortunately most of my clients have plumbing.

"What people don't know is that with proper service . . . well, I don't have to bore you with this. By the way, thanks for the invitation. June. I've got it marked in my calendar. Sounds like a good idea."

"June?" Toshio asked Tahara after Itoh hung up.

"Shibata said he had cleared it with you," Tahara said, "the party."

"Of course." Toshio turned to the intercom, "Mitsue," he said, "a basket of fruit for Hiroto Itoh. Sign the card Diamond Advertising and be sure to tell Saeki it's going out." He cut her off. "I don't know about the speaker phone, Tahara. What do you think?"

"I think that Hiroto Itoh sure has some kind of voice," Tahara said.

"You should hear him when he doesn't know who's on the other end of the line." Toshio looked at the couch against the wall. He felt like having a small metal sign made up, "This couch paid for by Hiroto Itoh and Company." He could do the same through the rest of the office—put signs up with the clients' names on them—through the rest of his life.

"I think it's funny," Tahara said, "that Mr. Itoh would say advertising is a dirty business. I mean . . ." He looked at Toshio for approval.

"Don't worry about Hiroto Itoh," Toshio said. "The only thing his hands touch is money."

Tahara stood up to go.

Toshio surveyed the accumulated mess on his desk. "Just a minute," he said, "can you understand this?" He had circled a Chinese character he couldn't read on one of the papers. Even in context. Neither could Tahara.

Okay, he thought, a lot to do. There was a product sample sitting in the far provinces of his desk. "The shampoo," Toshio said, "what's happening with that?"

"We're having a hard time finding the right approach," Tahara replied.

"What's the hang-up?" Toshio asked.

Tahara shrugged.

"Who's handling it?"

"Yamamoto."

"Yamamoto," Toshio said, "why did we do that?"

"I don't know," Tahara replied.

Toshio picked up the shampoo to check the labeling. "Yamamoto," he said half to himself. He looked at the packaging and then at Tahara. "Let's change the instructions. Instead of having people wash their hair every other day, have them wash their hair every single day. That'll increase sales."

Tahara smiled.

Toshio nodded. Change the instructions, turn up the volume. Add sugar to packaged foods. In special situations: reduce contents but increase the price. Toshio thought about how far one could go on a few principles judiciously applied. "And raise the minimum on the baseball pool," he said. "I'm through."

Tahara smiled again. "Will do," he said and stood up to leave.

Toshio could see the figure of Miho, one of his office ladies moving through the bull pen behind Tahara's silhouette in the door. He had been more aware of Miho lately; how he had overlooked her before he didn't know.

Yuko had been away on an island shoot. His calls to her had been left unanswered. Anyway, he told himself, in lieu of something solid it was just as well to have a few interests floating. "I need Yamamoto," Toshio said to Mitsue over the intercom.

"He's not here."

"Where is he?"

"He went to the dentist."

"Again?" Repeated trips to a dentist for treatment were common, but this was too much. Yamamoto's weakness for the high life was showing through once more. About every six months or so another round: drinking, gambling, women. It was one of Toshio's most difficult office problems, what to do about Yamamoto. The office welfare case. Most days, Toshio reminded himself, Yamamoto was normal as could be. Over all the years, Yamamoto had come to the office actually drunk only once. Toshio would never forget that day, at the salarymen's meeting. "Merry Christmas," Yamamoto had said. In his anger Toshio had asked him to clear his desk and leave, but during the ensuing delay Toshio felt strangely guilty. Yamamoto was part of the team too. Who knows what pressures he was under? Toshio had not been able to follow through.

Toshio had once suggested a couple months for Yamamoto at a Zen temple with no loss of pay in order to clear his mind. Toshio hoped that Yamamoto might be able to make a fresh start, to regain his equilibrium amid whatever difficulties he was facing. Yamamoto had accepted the offer—"To refresh my soul," as he put it—but the time in the temple had not helped. In fact, things had degenerated further. Toshio chided himself for not having supervised the selection of the temple more closely. Afterwards he had learned that the priests at Yamamoto's chosen temple had a reputation for drinking themselves. The temples were busy with businessmen, Toshio knew, all kinds of sales meetings and retreats. So he took responsibility for the failure. If only he had been thinking . . . after all, he had seen the beer deliveries to the temples too.

Give Yamamoto time off, that didn't work. Give him responsibility, that didn't work. Take away responsibility, that hadn't worked either. He'd had a clear chance to fire him and he had been unable to take it. Yamamoto had too much seniority to discuss it actively among the other salarymen, so during these periods Toshio dealt with the situation by pretending as if Yamamoto did not exist. Toshio would say at least one thing for Yamamoto. He did not come in on payday or the day before payday all buttoned-up and shiny. Toshio had seen those kinds. And neither did Yamamoto make a special effort to rally before the semiannual bonus. Toshio had actually come to Yamamoto with the envelope on several occasions and found himself apologizing for giving it to him late. Yamamoto did not discriminate. If he was going to take off, he took off. Toshio had a hard time getting angry at Yamamoto. It was easier to get mad at himself.

Toshio took a deep breath and thought. The families were getting together that night. A weekly visit to the parents that happily seemed to have developed into a biweekly or even monthly visit. It was one area where he and Nozomi shared complete, if unspoken, agreement: minimizing contact with his parents. But he remembered he had to pick up a present. They had not escaped that obligation.

Ordinarily Nozomi would have bought the gift, just as ordinarily the family would have met on a Sunday. Toshio and Nozomi had made a little bet, however. Toshio would buy the present if Nozomi could arrange to have the get-together set up on a weeknight. That way he could still make a golf date on Sunday and it limited the time actually spent with his parents from about seven hours to three. It wasn't easy to accomplish this because of school; he was surprised that Nozomi had been able to do it.

Toshio had not made a lunch appointment so he walked over to one of the department stores by the train station and then headed immediately to its gourmet and prepared food sections in the basement. Toshio knew that the first thing in the morning, when the store was less crowded and when the employees, including managers, lined up to greet customers, was a more convenient time. And he knew that just before closing, when stores dropped prices to clear perishables, was a good time too. But lunchtime was his favorite. He liked to go down to the basement and play a game by seeing how much of a meal he could make out of sampling the various foods.

Toshio tried not to be too obvious. Store employees were trained to turn free samples into sales. So Toshio asked questions, feigned surprise, checked prices and kept moving. First with the appetizers and the salads. Then with the fried foods, the meats and the imported foods. Toshio tried a few cookies and even some ice cream, and then drank a half cup of coffee before arriving in the fruit section. Fruit was a safe gift. It would be used, enjoyed. And everybody would know how much money he spent. But there were no samples there. And the prices were high. Toshio thought it was funny that in a country supposedly so well-known for its low inflation that everything was so expensive.

Toshio liked to say that if he could sell imported sweet potatoes on the street for three weeks he could retire with the proceeds. Or if he could import papayas and mangoes from Taiwan or the Philippines. Too bad, he mused, his brother was not a thinker. Toshio decided to pick up a hothouse muskmelon in the specially marked wooden box. For the price of four of these muskmelons he could have purchased a color television set.

Toshio would go directly to his parents, that was the plan. Included would be his brother and his family. In fact, his nephew's seventh birthday was the reason given for the event.

In the late afternoon, at what could only be described as the absolute last minute, however, the reputed fashion photographer genius Hideo Ota called Tahara to say that he had scheduled studio space for a two-hour rehearsal shoot with Yuko. Ota had met and worked with Yuko on the island travel campaign for another advertising agency. Toshio was extremely annoyed. True, the client had been demanding to see something soon, but where was there any semblance of proper notice here? And what was a rehearsal shoot?

Tahara reported that Ota had said it was simply a matter of being able to make the arrangements, that studio space was hard to get and that at the last minute it had become available. Why delay further? Toshio had a clearer inkling. Somehow he knew that Ota had taken a definite disliking to him. The two had only worked together once before and the work had been good. Toshio didn't know what he had done or said and Tahara wouldn't say anything about it, but Toshio could sense that Ota didn't like him. Toshio couldn't say that he really liked Ota either. Diamond Advertising was using him because the client had specifically requested his services and because his work was good. Toshio wondered if Ota had said anything about any of this to Yuko. After all, he and Yuko had not spoken recently.

Toshio wanted to go to the rehearsal session, then he wanted not to go. He was anxious about the whole affair, he knew the delay had irritated the client. His first instincts were to cancel with his parents, but he had begged out of so many of these occasions. . . . He decided to pass on the

96

session with Yuko and Ota, to keep his arrangement with Nozomi and the date with his parents. What could he add to the photo session? He knew he would hardly be able to look at Yuko. Let Ota do his thing. God knows the firm was paying him enough. Better not to think about Yuko. Nozomi would be pleased that Toshio showed up. Tahara could call later and tell him how it went. These younger people seemed to be able to communicate better among themselves than he could. Hopefully everyone was working toward the same end.

In the train, however, other feelings surfaced. Toshio felt increasingly resentful. So it was his nephew's birthday, Toshio felt restrained from being where he wanted to be, where he was needed. Toshio had had children before his brother. Now he felt like he had to celebrate with his brother's as if to apologize for the fact. The whole thing was made worse on the train when he felt some man was trying to press up against his leg. Toshio had had this happen once before and he didn't like it.

On the way to his parent's house Toshio passed an old woman stooped over by age. Toshio had seen her several times before in the neighborhood. She gave him a big smile and greeting. She's always smiling, Toshio thought, why?

"Now that we have money, we worry about inflation," Toshio heard his brother say as he entered the house. His father agreed. Who has money? Toshio thought. He greeted the family. His mother, his father, his brother and his wife, their two children impeccably dressed and seated. Arriving at his parents was never a comfortable moment. If he was late, he felt like he was early. If he was early, he felt like he was late. If he was on time, he felt like it was the wrong time.

Toshio handed the melon to his mother who set the package down and resumed the monologue Toshio had apparently interrupted. Specifically she was carrying on about one of the neighborhood children. A boy so overweight and without prospects that in its embarrassment his family had begun to rationalize the situation by claiming he would become a sumo wrestler.

Specifically, Toshio's mother discussed the boy. More generally her dialogue continued, her major theme being disapproval, and her minor theme, in Toshio's presence, inevitably developing that somewhere down the line Toshio had lost control. Perhaps even a conscious decision he had made to spite his parents, but that early on Toshio had taken his life out of their hands: his obstinacy as a child, his lack of application in school. Toshio's mother recalled the time Toshio had forgotten his briefcase on the bullet train and by the time he realized his mistake the briefcase had traveled to Kyushu, the southern island. His mother stressed the impermanence of business and Toshio's lack of service to the community. The high point to any of these tirades was to retell the story of how Toshio had once rear-ended a school bus. If there was ever a matter of something questionable going on in society the family turned to Toshio. His brother Kazuo, on the other hand, was the family's spokesperson for order, positive development and anything that stood for progress. Even in areas that had nothing to do with his supposed expertise in foreign affairs, Mrs. Matsuzaka would ask Kazuo a question and all eyes would turn his way. "I wish that Toshio had gone into the service," she once said, the popularity of the armed forces being such that those few who did work for the military generally chose to commute in civilian clothing.

She turned to Kazuo. "I notice a lot of construction in the city these days."

"It's a good time to build," Kazuo said.

"I thought so."

Toshio's attention had wandered. "Are you thinking about getting into that too?" she asked.

Toshio looked at his brother, thinking a few questions of his own. Why don't we buy more fruit from the Philippines? And why with all the gear around here do we license so few FM stations?

Nozomi arrived with Sanae. Toshio looked at his slightly disheveled wife and daughter. They were late. Good for Nozomi, he thought.

His mother barely acknowledged them. "The phone company called," she said to Kazuo. "They want to change our number. I don't see why they need to do that, do you?"

"They must have a reason," Kazuo said.

"I don't know," his mother said. "I wish somebody would do something about this. Your father won't."

"I don't know if it will accomplish anything," Kazuo said, "but I'll look into it for you."

"I wish someone would," she said.

Hideki arrived latest of all because of baseball practice. He was now taking a one-year break from *juku*. Toshio had worked out the details with Coach Shimazaki over a few beers in a neighborhood bar.

"Why are they making you play baseball?" his grand-mother asked.

"I want to play baseball."

"You didn't want to go to *juku* at first either. Have you ever heard of such a thing?" she asked her husband.

"No, I haven't." He paused before turning to Toshio. "There was an article in this morning's paper about cable television. That sounds like something you might want to look into."

The women stood up, almost in unison, to go into the kitchen.

Toshio's father began to expound on the potential of cable television. His conversation was intelligent, but he rambled. In the middle of one sentence he yawned in Toshio's face. He didn't yawn when Toshio was speaking. That would have been directly rude.

To Toshio it was just as simple: while I'm talking and have you in my control I can do as I please. Toshio excused himself and headed for the bathroom.

Passing the kitchen he heard his mother tell Nozomi, "You have everything." At least she let Nozomi into the kitchen. For years his mother had perpetuated the tradition of making the kitchen only her own and her eldest daughter-in-law's territory. Ridiculous in any case, Toshio thought, since all three had their own kitchens now.

Why couldn't the members of his family relax? he wanted to know. But then he had never had any luck changing their behavior. For that matter, he never had much luck changing his own. *Ubasuteyama,* he thought to himself, at sixty years of age, when parents were led to the top of a mountain and left to die. No one could be absolutely sure that parents had been abandoned in this way, but whether *ubasuteyama* had actually occurred or not, it was definitely there in the cultural mythos. Something doesn't have to happen often, or even regularly, Toshio knew, to hold an important place in the consensus mind. He could see evidence around him all the time. The business of trying to steal a feel on the train, the S&M in the comic books, the dramatic preoccupation with suicide, though suicide rates were not that high, and even now as he listened to his mother, his own thoughts about *ubasuteyama.*

"How was practice?" Toshio asked Hideki when he sat down again. To hell with his parents, to hell with his brother. He had his own family. He could start there. Hideki was looking strong these days. Had a bit of the buck in him. There hadn't been any talk about eyeglasses lately.

"Practice was fine," Hideki said.

"What did you work on?" Toshio asked.

"N hing really," Hideki said. "Coach just had us do a few things."

Toshio looked around the room. They might be a family unit, but it sure was hard to have a conversation with any of the members individually. With his own parents he understood the frustration. With his brother too. But neither was it so easy with his own son.

The phone rang.

"For me?" Toshio asked.

"Yes," his mother said. Everyone turned to watch him take the call.

"Tahara, why are you calling me so early?"

"Something happened," Tahara said. "I had to let you know."

"What happened?" Toshio asked.

"With the cigarette lighter," Tahara said, "Miss Tanioka's dress caught on fire."

"My God," Toshio said. He knew he should have been there. It was his punishment for not being there. "Is she all right?"

"She's all right," Tahara said, "although I think she was really scared. She said she never expected it would be like this."

"Of course not," Toshio said. "Neither did we. What happened?"

"It's hard to explain."

"Try," Toshio said.

Tahara was not making sense.

"What did Hideo Ota say?" Toshio interrupted.

"Ota was thrilled with the shoot," Tahara said. "He said that if the proofs come out he'll use them as they are. He said that Tanioka is a natural, that when people see this on top of the island travel campaign she's going to get a lot of notice."

Hideo Ota is an asshole, Toshio thought. He probably did this on purpose. First there was the PTA and Big Catch Sushi. Now an ad for a cigarette lighter where the girl's dress catches on fire . . . the local Fire Safety Council.

"But what happened?" Toshio asked. "Tell me exactly."

"Her dress caught on fire," Tahara said. "She tried to take it off, but Ota kept on shooting. A lot of men on the set ran to help her put out the fire, but Ota kept shooting. She wasn't hurt at all, it really wasn't that big a fire. Ota said that the synthetic material in her dress made for a bigger effect. He said that the whole thing could come out great."

"Where is everyone now?"

"We're winding down."

"Yuko must be mad at Ota," Toshio said.

"I don't think so," Tahara said. "Ota said that it went great."

She's probably mad at me, he thought. "Is she there?"

"She's here, but I think she's in her dressing room."

"They didn't have to call in any outside help, did they?"

"Ota wanted to," Tahara said, "but there was no need. Don't worry, please. I just called to let you know."

"I'm coming down to the studio," Toshio said. "I should have been there from the beginning."

"Oh," Tahara said.

"Oh what?" Toshio asked.

"I'm not sure we'll be here."

"Where are you going?"

"They're talking about going out for a drink."

"A drink?" Toshio asked. "Where?"

"I don't think they've decided yet," Tahara said.

Toshio had the sinking feeling he had known since childhood—that somewhere else, without him, someone was having a good time. He would miss it this time too.

The visit defied termination. Twice they started to leave, twice as if by divine power his mother froze them into place. Nozomi did skillfully avoid her mother-in-law's several attempts to schedule another date as soon as possible. Nozomi had learned that there was no satisfying her mother-in-law. Fulfilling one obligation seemed only to create another. The best thing was to delay, buy time, postpone.

The family took a taxi home, quietly. There was a transition period they had come to accept following difficult visits. Looking at the four of them, an outsider might have mistakenly concluded that they fought among themselves. But the immediate nuclear family was together on this one. They just needed time to themselves to work it out of their systems.

Reiko called Nozomi in the morning to say that the cafe bar was progressing. She was making decisions as to menu, layout, prices. More important, she implied, were all the men she was meeting, how attractive they were and how things were developing, if only below the surface. "You have to be careful," she told Nozomi. "You sleep with a man once and he falls in love with you."

Conversation turned to the weather, which had remained uncharacteristically hot and with a mugginess associated only with the worst part of the rainy season. Reiko asked if the public swimming pools for children would open early, but Nozomi knew that regardless of the weather the pool would open on July 1, according to schedule.

The conversation drifted, but then Nozomi had some news of her own. Maybe not momentous news, but important enough to her. She had decided to resume English study, specifically to take private lessons in conversation. Responding to an ad she had seen in one of the English-language newspapers, Nozomi had taken out her dictionary and composed a short note to Marcia Sloan, the name given, and sent it off. She liked the feel of the ad, although she wondered if her English was really good enough to tell. The ad had some vitality, character. It was an American woman and Nozomi could see from the address listed that she was staying not far away.

When Marcia Sloan phoned several days later, in spite of the fact that she was pleasant and had even known a little Japanese, they had a horrendously frustrating time of scheduling their first meeting. The telephone call brought out the worst of Nozomi's fears. That she had forgotten what little she knew, that her teacher would think she was stupid, and that in the end she could not learn English. She was annoyed with herself for not having had someone else who spoke English better, even from Toshio's office, make the arrangements for her as a go-between. Still, she reminded herself, they had been able to make the appointment. The days passed quickly. It was not long until 11:15 a.m. on the Saturday of their first meeting. Nozomi had heard that Americans liked using quarter hour times to set up appointments. She thought it was funny.

Marcia Sloan arrived on time. She was a tall, thin woman of twenty-four who had come to Japan with her boyfriend on graduation from NYU. Marcia had majored in film and had written her thesis comparing the work of the famed directors Akira Kurosawa and Yasujiro Ozu. Many, many times watching those movies in the United States Marcia had felt a special identification with the Japanese. Knowing that she could support herself by teaching English, it had seemed like a fine opportunity. And in retrospect, she thought, it had

104

all worked out pretty well—if only her boyfriend hadn't split.

Sanae peeked down from upstairs but chose to take the back way out. Nozomi felt nervous herself. She offered coffee.

Marcia asked for Japanese tea. "I don't drink coffee," she said.

They sat down. Marcia considered taking out the note Nozomi had written in response to the ad to show her a couple of corrections, but thought better of it. The lesson could take its own pace. She had been through this many times. In the beginning would be a lead-in period of "Twenty Questions." Marcia had heard these questions so often that she had thought about printing answers.

1. "How old are you?"
   "Twenty-four."
2. "Are you married?"
   "No."
3. "Why not?"
   "I haven't found the right person yet."
4. "What was your purpose in coming to Japan?"
   "I had been interested for a long time and I wanted to see it for myself."
5. "Do you like Japan?"
   "Very much."
6. "Can you eat Japanese food?"
   "Yes."
7. "Do you like Japanese food?"
   "I like it, although it's a little sweet sometimes."
8. "What other parts of Japan have you seen?"
   "I've been to Kyoto and Hiroshima. I'd like to visit Hokkaido."
9. "Where are you from in America?"
   "Long Island—New York."

10. "Do you have any brothers and sisters?"
"I have one brother and one sister. Both younger."
11. "Are your parents living in New York?"
"Yes."
12. "Have they been to Japan?"
"No, but they would like to come."
13. "Your parents must miss you."
"Yes, but we write a lot of letters."
14. "How long will you stay in Japan?"
"I don't know."
15. "What will you do when you return?"
"I don't know yet."
16. "When will you get married?"
"I don't know that either."
17. "Would you marry a Japanese?"
"Definitely, the person is the key."
18. "Did you study Japanese before you came here?"
"I wish I had."
19. "How does Japan differ from the image you had when you were in America?"
"It's safer and more organized. Very different. People told me that Japan was just trying to be like the United States. But I don't think so."
20. "What's it like in your country now?"
"My country is asleep."

Marcia was fairly impressed with Nozomi's English. She was rusty, but she had some ability to communicate. Comprehension was especially difficult, that was to be expected, but when they would get stuck Marcia could write down the word and Nozomi often knew. Some of the mistakes Nozomi made Marcia could have predicted. In describing how she wanted to deal with holidays Nozomi said "case by case" instead of "depending on." In discussing their lesson she said "man to man" instead of "one to one."

106

In themselves these were not important mistakes. What was interesting to Marcia was that so many people made them. With the same textbooks in use all across the country, if a mistake or misusage was included it tended to be reflected in people's speech everywhere.

For Nozomi it was hard enough to understand Marcia as it was, but then every time she thought she did understand it seemed that Marcia was taking the opportunity to express an opinion or to ask for one. "What do you think?" she kept asking. The whole thing was intimidating, not to mention the way Marcia carried herself, the way she moved, the way she gestured. It was free and flexible, but at the same time aggressive and not especially graceful. Marcia took great pains to make sure the financial arrangements, including pay for canceled lessons, were understood. Nozomi thought it was unnecessary to dwell on this.

"I've been through this too many times," Marcia said, "so I want to make it clear. By the way," she added, "I've been thinking about leaving the school where I work. If you know of anybody else who might want to study English, please let me know."

Nozomi smiled, although leaving a job was not something she would brag about.

Toshio returned as Marcia was leaving; he had come home a little early hoping to see the new English teacher. "See you again," he said.

"See you again," Marcia said.

"How was it?" Toshio asked when she had left.

"Difficult," Nozomi said. "I could hardly understand a word she was saying."

"Aren't you going to use a textbook?" Toshio asked.

"She said that I could use the public television station magazines and practice with their programs."

"That sounds like a good idea."

107

Hideki appeared at the door.

Toshio looked at his watch. "You're early."

"You're home early too," Hideki replied.

"No practice today?" Toshio asked.

"We have our first game this week," Hideki said. "Coach said we should take it easy."

"When's the game?" Toshio asked. "I'd like to make it."

"Dad, I may not even play."

"Son, I'm not trying to . . ."

There was another knock at the door. The Seiko Matsuda look-alike, Hideki's friend, the girl with the envelope. She wore a UCLA T-shirt. Her friend stood back by the gate.

"Excuse me," she said and offered what looked like long underwear, shorts and socks. They were clean, pressed and had been neatly folded. "Coach Shimazaki said we should take them out to the team members."

Hideki blushed. He could not move to take them.

Nozomi accepted the clothing instead. "Won't you come in?" she asked.

"Thank you," the girl said, "but we can't. Excuse me." She bowed to leave.

"Who's that?" Toshio asked Hideki when the girls had gone. She looked so much like Seiko Matsuda.

"Some girls volunteered to help with the team."

Nozomi went into the kitchen to grab some fruit. Hideki went upstairs. "Nozomi," Toshio yelled. "Imagine! Seiko Matsuda is ironing Hideki's underwear!"

Nozomi rushed past her husband and out the front door. She caught up with the girls on the street and gave them the fruit. Nozomi liked this girl, the way she acted, the way she came to their house. She was exactly the kind of girl she wanted for her son. Unafraid. Unburdened. And that smile, Nozomi thought. Her smile reminds me of a time when I was happy.

108

SIX

T oshio did not know whether to be thrilled or concerned when Takashi Muraoka insisted on coming up to the office. Muraoka worked for Maruichi Bank, the lead bank for both Aoki Chemical and Hiroto Itoh's firm. Itoh had said many times that he did not believe in borrowing money, but the bank evidently believed in keeping his account. Itoh was pulling strings on Toshio's behalf, because, aside from his position of influence within the bank, Muraoka happened also to be son-in-law to the president of Aoki Chemical. His visit meant that Diamond Advertising was still in the running. In a panic Toshio had assembled a meeting of the salarymen to determine how best to present themselves. It was decided to play down voluminous research and statistics as alienating and to stress instead the "boutique" nature of Diamond Advertising—that being small the firm was able to respond quickly and personally to its clients' needs. Service. Diamond Advertising had not hesitated to involve itself in controversy or with problem clients and was on the move. A fact underscored by Toshio's recent first hiring of a Tokyo University graduate. So much for the presentation. "Then take him out to get laid," a voice in the back had said.

Things were happening. Indeed, that this Tokyo University graduate, Shinichi Aihara, had decided to join Diamond Advertising was in itself a milestone. True, Toshio had offered up, paying far more than an established company would have had to in order to land someone of the same standing—in the process upsetting his own salary scale and seniority system. Unable to conceal what might have been the beginnings of a two-tiered salary system, Toshio had presented it to the salarymen as a means of getting some computer expertise into the office. Aihara's background was in statistics and computers. The men had taken it surprisingly well, as if they realized the time had come. Aihara himself had proved to be more of a challenge. He seemed to own only one business suit, was apparently working off his own office schedule and occasionally locked himself in the computer room without responding. Of equal concern were the repeated calls he was now taking from photographer Hideo Ota, who had spent three weeks at Tokyo University himself once and who seemingly had decided to avoid Toshio completely and to communicate with Aihara and Tahara instead. His first week in the office Aihara had presented to the salarymen at an afternoon meeting a paper entitled "The Changing Face of Japanese Advertising" in which he challenged the firm to be more aggressive in the future and to consider the possibility, perhaps the necessity, of promoting its own talent.

As Toshio reviewed his salarymen, the words "mixed grill" came to mind. There was Saeki, who couldn't drink. Yamamoto, who did. Tahara, the office English specialist who couldn't speak English. Shibata. Now there was Aihara.

Toshio gave Muraoka a tour of the office personally. "This is where we seat our Tokyo University graduates," he said, the satisfaction of being able to say it worth every yen

110

he was paying Aihara for the privilege. But Aihara had locked the door again. "Open up," Toshio called and knocked.

"Tokyo University," Muraoka said, "the ivory tower. That's very impressive."

Aihara opened the door.

"To be honest," Toshio said to Muraoka, "half the time I don't understand what they're doing myself."

Aihara smiled and turned to the keyboard. "The casino program is running again, Chief," he said.

"Very funny, Aihara," Toshio said, escorting Muraoka out of the computer room. Shibata looked like he was about to fall asleep at his desk.

"Service," Toshio said to Muraoka, "service is so important." They walked into his office.

"Hiroto Itoh," Mitsue said on the intercom.

"Good." Toshio picked up. "Mr. Itoh, I'm going to put you on my speaker phone now. I have someone you know in my office—Takashi Muraoka."

"Muraoka," Itoh bellowed, "it's about time you got together with Diamond Advertising."

"Why don't you come into the city so we can discuss it?" Muraoka was not sure how he should be directing his voice, so he was taking command instead by placing his hands on both sides of Toshio's desk and yelling straight ahead.

"I can hardly hear you," Itoh said. "What's happening with the account?"

"We like what we've seen so far," Muraoka said. "We may need some follow-up."

Toshio smiled at Muraoka. If your greed doesn't exceed our enthusiasm, he thought. He didn't like Muraoka. He could place him immediately. The type who substitutes authority for intelligence, style for understanding.

Toshio could sense the disappointment coming on. A bank would never recommend his type of agency to a major client. Regardless of the merits Diamond Advertising would never get the account. It was nice of Hiroto Itoh to be pushing, but it didn't matter. It just obligated Toshio to entertain this man. Sure there had been a lot of new faces around lately, but for what? They were all along the same lines, the same practiced relationships.

Some voices in the background on Itoh's end. "Well," they could hear Itoh saying, "if the vacuum isn't working on that truck have the men take another truck." He came back to the phone. "Sorry, where were we?"

"Itoh," Muraoka yelled, "do you clean up rivers?" The men laughed.

Voices in the background again. "He did what?" Itoh asked. He came back to the phone. "I'm sorry, a few things to take care of on this end."

"We'll talk to you later," Muraoka said.

"Soon."

Toshio looked at Muraoka and thought back to the first time he had entertained Hiroto Itoh. At the time, Itoh's company had represented the same kind of quantum leap for Diamond Advertising that Aoki Chemical did now. Itoh and Toshio had begun with a few drinks. Toshio remembered that Itoh had hardly cracked a smile. He talked about the challenge of sales, the necessity of watching local politics, the importance of maintaining good labor/management relations. He said that he didn't believe in borrowing money and that until recently he had felt the same way about advertising. "Why should we use it?"

Toshio looked him directly in the eye. "Some people think you vacuum shit for a living," he said, "but you don't. You clean people's homes."

"What else can I show you?" Toshio asked Muraoka.

112

"How about the bathroom?"

"I'll show you."

The two men went into the bathroom. Muraoka stepped up to the urinal and really hugged it. Wasn't Muraoka afraid he would get his clothing wet? Walking back toward the office Toshio couldn't see a drop on Muraoka, but looking at his own pants he noticed that he had leaked.

"What would you like to do tonight?" Toshio asked. "Start with a bite of dinner?"

"I don't think I'm too hungry."

"Of course," Toshio responded, "maybe something to drink."

"I don't go to the eye doctor when my foot hurts," Muraoka said. "You'd be surprised how hard it is to enjoy a little old-fashioned fun anymore."

Toshio understood. Muraoka wasn't referring to geishas. Muraoka was an ass man. Toshio thought about calling Ken Kondo—Ken Kondo, the pussy commander. Ken always knew where the best new places were.

Toshio could feel his pulse quickening. There was no need to ask twice. It was a fever he had caught as a young man on the streets of Tokyo, unable then to do much about it. In his youth he had taken to other antics in order to relieve his curiosity. If he'd he had a sister perhaps the whole business would have seemed less mysterious, but he didn't have a sister. His mother had been no help. Left with the comic books on the train and the press of the crowd, Toshio had developed other strategies, other schemes. Walking the streets of areas he would have liked to penetrate he pretended he was a newspaper boy, a messenger, a delivery boy, carrying his ruse long enough to gain entrance, to catch a feel of those houses, of the shows, of the women. A smell of the streets in the days when he had nothing, no money, no pride and no future.

Toshio remembered his mentor at Diamond Advertising, Goro Nagai. Nagai had originally interviewed him, kept an eye out for him. Those were not the days of two percent unemployment. A job meant more. Nagai had taken it upon himself to guide Toshio, protect him. And he introduced him to the nightlife. Sometimes with clients, sometimes alone. It was a world Toshio had longed for, looked for without entry. His own personal life at the time had consisted of little more than what he thought were unsuccessful attempts to get Nozomi, the girl in the department store, to pay attention to him. Each day he saw her working, each day a little more tired. It had motivated him to work harder, fired his intensity to take her out of there. But at the time he was hardly able to speak with her, much less touch her. And if he had tried to touch her, he could have considered it the end to any chance he did have with her.

Nagai was a character. Toshio absorbed his every word. "One dog barks at nothing and ten thousand spread it as truth," he said. "Feed a dog for three days and he's grateful for three years. Feed a cat for three years, but stop—he's grateful for three days."

Nagai was always pointing things out. "In the subways or the trains," he said, "when a rider unknowingly overpays, do the ticket takers call it out? What happens to that money?" There were so many things that Toshio had never noticed. "We fought the Second World War with one-eightieth the industrial capacity of the United States," Nagai said. "What do you think about that?"

Toshio marveled that for all his insight Nagai was such a poor businessman. He seemed to know about the world in one way, but when it came to the fundamentals of advertising, even after so many years in the business, Nagai was a disaster. In practical terms he seemed to know only one thing, although he knew it well. He knew how to enjoy himself. It was a partnership that had benefits for both. Toshio increasingly covered for Nagai in the office, doing the work of both men ostensibly under Nagai's supervision. Nagai tutored Toshio in the subtleties of after-hours life. Toshio could recall the first place they had entered as if it was the one single event in his life that preceded every other. She was an older woman. Older anyway than he told himself he would have liked. But she managed to relax him. Set him down on the bench with steam towels, somehow made her body attractive to him, made him want her. Made him want her, but hadn't given. She just massaged, it seemed for so long. And then finally she took him into her mouth. He could remember it clearly. This is great, he thought.

Toshio's response and enthusiasm seemed to fire Nagai. Work increasingly became a footnote to their personal crusade for release. Nagai found in Toshio the son he never had. Toshio found the teacher, the attention, even the love. Those days when there was a choice Nagai always let Toshio take the prettier girl, but Nagai always seemed to have the better time. Toshio had to learn against his nature. To slow down, to rest, to relax. Not necessarily lessons he learned well.

The favorite times Toshio enjoyed with Nagai must have been at the old road shows, the "black and white" shows. There were also "white" shows, meaning all women, but it was the black and white shows—men and women—he liked the best. Sometimes for the finale there would be seven or eight girls on stage. There was usually a girl who did a strip version of a traditional dance. There was a girl who would come out and let members of the audience finger her. There was a girl who would pour a glass of sake for anyone who would buy a book of discounted tickets for future shows. And there was Won. The dog named Won. Won and his mistress. "Aooooh," Nagai and Toshio had barked across the office to each other. The way Won smiled as he was putting it to her. Won had become a legend of the night. There were the various acts, including Won and his mistress, and there were the girls who fucked. Toshio had once seen three men from the audience get up on stage to get laid at the same time. Actually, he had seen two. He'd been the third.

Alone Toshio might have stayed at these shows for thirty minutes, forty minutes, an hour. With Nagai they stayed for two or three hours. Toshio missed him now more than he liked to admit. Toshio might have said it was the times that had changed and lost their intensity, their edge, but he didn't know that. He did know that he had always seemed to have a better time with Nagai. He was sorry that Nagai had not lived to see him take over the office. When he died, Toshio stepped in quietly to pay his gambling debts, then sent money, not large sums, but regularly to Nagai's family until his daughter married.

"Two sushi chefs with the same tuna are equally skilled with the knife," Nagai had said, "but one chef always produces more delicious sushi. Why?" Toshio wished he could hear him say it now. "It's how you handle the tuna," Nagai said, "this is the trick. How you handle the tuna."

"Know any good places around here?" Muraoka intruded on Toshio's reverie.

"We're here," Toshio said. The pink salon was dimly lit and had Christmas ornaments hanging around the room. Booths were arranged and partitioned in such a way that with the poor lighting, unless Toshio actually poked his head into another booth, regardless of what might be going on, he couldn't tell much more than that the booth was occupied. Toshio paid a cover charge on entrance. The first thing the cover charge revealed was how attractive the girls might be. While there were no absolutes, it was pretty well established

116

that the more one was willing to pay the more likely one would find his "type."

Toshio liked pink salons. Most of the time, he had learned about sex-for-sale, it was important to put the woman in control, not always easy when having sex on a first meeting, one-time basis. Inside a pink salon, however, Toshio was not going to get laid. He was going to get a blow job or a hand job. Toshio had found that even this allowed the girls to retain more sense of control. Maybe it wasn't the highest high, but he'd had some pretty good times there nonetheless.

Toshio and Muraoka split up. Toshio liked the slight delay and resulting anticipation about who might join him in the booth. He was never sure what he was going to find in a pink salon. Toshio had met the best there, every so often going so far as to pay something extra to take a girl out. Toshio knew to be careful in those situations. Some girls did nothing but generate enthusiasm and then once outside they would wilt. Toshio wondered who might join him. He hadn't been able to see much upon entering the place.

Finally she arrived. A disappointment. Chunky and not especially attractive. "Beer?" she asked.

Toshio hoped she was just taking orders, but her outfit—American wild west with belt, stockings and red silk panties—suggested otherwise. He was willing to bail out. "Muraoka," he called, "all right?"

"All right?" Muraoka responded, "Great place!" Toshio was stuck. His girl poured him a beer and tried to engage him in conversation. Toshio could not muster much interest. He knew the pattern well, knew what she would do, how he would respond. She would touch him on his thigh a few times. She would ask him if he wanted her to go and play.

"Go where?" he would respond.

She would have a hard time of it with him. Finally she would get discouraged and talk to one of the men who were supervising the place. The manager would come over and ask Toshio if the girl was perhaps not his type. Toshio would grunt and the manager would ask him about what his type was, the specifics.

Young and thin, Toshio would say.

But this girl was hanging around too long. She motioned with her hand. "Would you like me to?" she asked.

"I can do that myself," Toshio replied. Was the place shorthanded for the night? The beer was going, the girl was still around. Time was passing. She brought him another beer.

The alcohol helped. It didn't make him want her, but it did work to open up his mind. He would not have admitted it, but he had been facing new feelings lately. It seemed like every magazine he looked at had some article related to what was called "feeling couple"—the ideal relationship. Or some article on the new feminism. He didn't approve or identify with these matters, but once introduced they were hard to avoid. What a mess the whole thing was becoming. Up until now men had their world. And women had theirs. Now Western morality and guilt were disrupting what had once seemed a less complicated aspect of life. Nowadays when entertaining it was important to be so much more careful about the other person's views. Especially the younger men. For himself, what could he say? There was no good solution. Like a poet had once written about eating the poisonous delicacy blowfish, "Those who eat are stupid. But those who don't eat are also stupid."

"Matsuzaka," he heard Muraoka call, "enjoying yourself?"

Not particularly, Toshio thought. "Finished?" he asked.

"Sure am," Muraoka replied.

"Then let's go," Toshio said. He was happy to pay the bill, didn't mind what it cost, just happy to get out of there. The men stumbled out onto the street. They walked quickly for several blocks but without destination. Finally they pulled up to rest at a street corner, but they were just standing around. "Is there someplace in particular you'd like to go?" Toshio asked.

"Any ideas?" Muraoka responded.

There were any number of places Toshio knew to go, but he hardly felt like wasting the good ones with Muraoka. The others he really wasn't interested in himself. He felt annoyed with the situation, having to spend the evening with this man. He took a deep breath and looked to the side to think. In the gutter he noticed a torn-off page from a sports paper. Toshio twisted for a better view but could hardly see the standings. "Look at this," he called Muraoka over, "I didn't realize the Giants were so far behind . . ."

His eyes strayed to a part of the next page that was also lying in the gutter. "High School Baseball Update, Coach Shimazaki to be shimazakied?" There was a short article Toshio could barely make out, lying as it was in the gutter. The article indicated that Coach Shimazaki had arranged a special game for his team with a major Osaka powerhouse coached by another former pro-ballplayer and long-standing friend. The game was scheduled for late May and would be telecast as the inaugural game of new "Saturday High School Game of the Week" coverage that had been initiated to capitalize on the success and popularity of the well-covered spring and fall national tournaments. Toshio read on. Shimazaki, the article reported, had succeeded in recruiting two former little league all-stars to join his team. He was not, the article speculated, intending to wait around. Of greater interest to Toshio, however, was the small poorly defined picture placed to the side of the article and labeled with the two all-stars' names. In the poor light and with the players' caps on it was hard to tell, but Toshio suspected there had been a mistake. One of the players looked a lot like Hideki.

"My son," Toshio said to Muraoka and explained while fishing the remnant out of the gutter so as to determine which newspaper it came from, "I think."

"That's great," Muraoka said.

"We just decided to let him play," Toshio said. "He never played before this season."

"No kidding," Muraoka said.

"No kidding," Toshio said. "We've played two games already."

"Celebrate?" Muraoka asked.

"Absolutely," Toshio said. "How 'bout a drink?"

"A drink?" Muraoka replied. "Just a drink? Why not go all the way?"

"Now?" Toshio asked. He thought about how many copies of the paper to buy.

"Why not?" Muraoka asked.

Because we just left the pink salon, Toshio thought. "Why not?" he said.

They found a newsstand nearby and then took a cab to the nearest district of what had formerly been called Turkish baths. Under protest from the Turkish government the Foreign Ministry had pressured these houses to change their names. What my brother does, Toshio thought, when every country in the world chooses nationalities other than its own after which to name its baths: Turkish, Thai, Swedish. Some places even called them Japanese. He didn't hear the government complaining about that. Now to avoid controversy these baths had taken on the safer name of "Soapland." They were housed in colorfully lit buildings whose architecture was a Disneyland of the imagination. There were windmills, castles, pagodas, bridges, staircases, blinking lights, and there were hustlers out front almost like

120

the ticket takers and hustlers in the parking lots. It reminded Toshio of something American he had seen once in a magazine: miniature golf courses.

The place was air-conditioned. Inside the men removed their shoes and were escorted to a lounge where they sat down. There was a coffee table in front of the couch with magazines on it. Reputable periodicals. Under and behind the sofa were the stroke books. While they waited the two men checked through the programs on a remote-controlled large-screen television set up in the room. There was the sports wrap-up. The late news. A girl was bouncing around on the television show "Eleven PM."

They turned to the video channel. There was a rape on the video channel.

As usual they suffered a short wait. Toshio wondered if all these places weren't linked by underground tunnel and when a guest or guests walked in if the girls didn't come running from a central waiting area somewhere else. The host came back and asked to know their type. Toshio could see the hint of a tattoo on his arm underneath his shirt. *Yakuza*. Sex, drugs, pornography, gambling, guns, protection, promotion.

Although some *Yakuza* brandished guns out of weakness, Toshio knew that guns and drugs were the clearest no's. Foreign women and underaged girls were also increasingly off-limits. Most other activities, if handled discretely, were tolerated. There was a growing need to treat the women somewhat fairly, at least the Japanese women. Otherwise they wouldn't stick around. So some made a lot of money now. "If I work in an office," one girl had told Toshio, "I make 900 yen an hour. If I work in a snack, I make 2000, maybe 2500. I work in one of these places I can make 10,000 or 15,000."

"What about your own life?" Toshio asked.

"What about it?" the girl replied. "This is not love."

"Boyfriend?"

"No."

Toshio persisted.

"Boys my age don't have money," she said.

"They have some money."

"Do they?"

Toshio knew it. Every society has a distribution of sex as well as a distribution of wealth—usually with a relationship between the two.

"Would you like a young girl or a technician?" their host asked.

"A young girl," Muraoka said.

The man turned to Toshio.

"Both."

Toshio had been to Turkish, Thai, Swedish and Japanese baths all over Asia, but he could not as yet resolve one question: when the lights were out did it all feel the same? He knew this much, he liked some of the other set-ups better. Where it was possible to see the women first, make a choice as to partner. In Soapland one was pretty much left to take whoever was introduced. It was possible for a man who knew the place or one girl in particular to make a request on entrance, and if really dissatisfied, a man could always ask for another girl. But the truth was there weren't many people Toshio would have liked to sit next to on a bus for eighty minutes, much less spend that time with them in bed. Whenever possible he liked to see the merchandise first.

Muraoka's girl came out. She winked at Toshio. She looked strangely familiar. Did he know her from another house? Several years before Toshio had seen a write-up complete with photographs and addresses in a magazine devoted to nightlife and entertainment. There had been one girl in particular he had followed up on. His first question at

122

the time—he had not been able to resist—"What do your parents think about having your picture in a magazine like that?"

"I didn't ask," she said.

Toshio had returned and inquired for her on several occasions since, but she had always been off. Or busy. Was this the same girl? He wasn't sure. One thing Toshio could say was that if it was the same girl Muraoka was in for a treat. That girl had been a real tiger with the eighty minutes. Toshio watched them disappear down the hall. He felt a little jealous. Even in this place, he wanted Muraoka's girl.

He waited for his own. Maybe she was running through the underground tunnels, he thought. Or some *Yakuza* member was making arrangements with her. In the beginning: "Would you like to wear pretty dresses and work with other girls?" Later the inducement to make a little money. Preparation and instruction from the other girls. More likely, Toshio knew, his girl was now busy cleaning herself after having been with another man.

Toshio's girl arrived in kimono. She led him to a room that looked like the examination room in a doctor's lust dream gone bad. In one corner on a small white metal chest, was a tray with oil, powder and tissue. Inside the chest, he guessed, were rubbers, perhaps a vibrator, maybe other things. Leave them for another man's experience. She looked at herself in the mirror.

Over here, he thought. He grabbed her.

"No," she said, "wait."

He could really hate women sometimes.

"I'm sorry," she said.

He was annoyed.

"I'm sorry, you scared me." She sat down on the bed. "Now," she said finally, "you can come here now." She unbraided her hair and let it fall, shook it loose.

"How old are you?" Toshio asked. This girl did know how to play with her hair.

"How old do you think I am?"

Toshio had a formula he used for guessing women's ages: make a real guess, divide by two and then add seven. She looked like she was twenty-six. Half was thirteen. Add seven. "Twenty?"

She was happy with his answer. "Twenty-two."

"No kidding," Toshio said. The younger the better.

She started to undress, but Toshio did not respond. "Why?" she asked finally.

"What do you mean?"

"Why are you here?"

"Why am I here?" he replied. "Why are you here?"

She laughed, then sat down again and kind of hunched over. She took a deep breath, rested her head on her hands and looked away. "Maybe it would be better if you took someone else."

It was unusual. On other occasions Toshio had found that girls would fight much harder to mask their feelings and carry on. Toshio's immediate reaction did include a sense of frustration. Even to be paying, even to be supposed to be getting it, and he was having trouble. Toshio reminded himself that he had placed himself in the situation, but still he had an inclination to walk her back and take someone else. Have someone else come running through the tunnels. Then as he began to listen to her . . . and her story was not much more than a laundry list of failure—family, marriage, money, school, job . . . an unexpected thing began to happen. He began to get an erection. If a businessman walks into my office and tells me he's messed up everything in his life, I wouldn't want to deal with him, Toshio thought. But a woman starts telling me that she's messed up her life and I want to go to bed with her. Even help her.

"I'm a prostitute," she said matter-of-factly as she folded back the sheets.

"Well, if you thought you might like to work in an advertising office, I don't know, I might . . ."

She laughed. "Come here," she said. "You think you can do anything you want with women? You think women are easy?"

If women were easy, he thought, why would we be going to these places? He took off his clothes and climbed in.

She put a rubber on him with her mouth. That was a good move, but so much for kissing. He'd had a fight with Nozomi once. Told her that she had bad breath after she had gone down on him. The girl worked him up quickly now, pulled him over and spread for him. It wasn't long. Coming, he felt his weakness. Even this whore, he thought, even this girl could take him. He rested.

She got up to go to the bathroom. He knew that she was cleaning herself, he could hear her gargling. When she came back he went into the bathroom. He felt a little tense. Even after all these years and any number of times. But this was a long way from standing next to a pretty girl on the subway, he told himself. A long way from the days when the choice on a business trip had been a nicer place to stay—or a dormitory with money left over for a hand job. A long way from the days when he would unplug his television set at a business hotel in order to save what portion of the coin he had put into the meter to buy an hour's worth of the regular fare or twenty minutes worth of pornography. A long way from the days when he would wait until after midnight for the cheaper rate at the love hotel. He used warm water to wash his hands. "Never touch a woman when your hands are cold," he could hear Nagai saying. He looked at the toilet sunk as it was in the floor. The toilet looked to him like a vagina.

After some time had passed he knew she would try to get him off again. This was not a cheap one-shot place. These girls made a lot of money and they worked for it. She would try to get him up. Usually he could, sometimes he couldn't. The truth was that he didn't have the energy he used to. She should wait, not start in too soon. As if they were fishing together. Wait, wait, waiting. He thought about Yuko. That helped. He could feel some blood rushing. Now Miho. Miho in the office. The balloon was filling. Yuko, Miho. He told himself not to move too quickly. Yuko, Miho, Nozomi. Nozomi? He tried to relax. To relax. He had learned. Not to try and make it until he was ready.

Toshio found himself thinking about Yuko and Miho now while she was working him with a hand job. The engine was turning, he was moving. He rolled her over onto her back and took her. It felt good. But now she wouldn't kiss him. He wanted to, but she wouldn't. "Shower?" she asked.

He knew the meaning of that song. Their time was up. He showered first. Afterwards she went into the bathroom. He could hear her coughing. Putting on his tie he noticed that the door to the bathroom was open just a crack; he could see she was cleaning herself. He was ready to go.

He paid while waiting for Muraoka who had yet to come out. It was a lot of money he was paying now, he thought. But when it was cheaper who could afford it?

He sat down in front of the television. Twice he started to drift off. Both times he found himself coming back with thoughts of *pachinko*. *Pachinko* of all things. Over and over he would watch the machine throw its balls up. Over and over they would fall down to their fate. To nothing. All the time spent. The obligation. Nothing. The constraint. Nothing. In the noise and the rhythm. "Nothing," the machine seemed to say. "You are nothing."

126

Muraoka came out. The two men nodded to each other, smiled and shook hands as if they had accomplished something. Muraoka invited Toshio out for a drink. Toshio was tired, he felt like calling it a night, but how hard it was to pass, to say no. Impossible. He couldn't pass. He was obligated.

Some small bars were located nearby. Small enough that they held only five or six people. Toshio knew one where they could drink. Whiskey. As they were sitting down he experienced a peculiar sensation. For an instant he felt like he could smell pussy everywhere. In the whiskey, in the water, the wood, the air.

Toshio looked at Muraoka. Muraoka was looking better. When Toshio folded the paper back to look at Hideki's picture, Muraoka slapped him on the back.

After sitting awhile the bar stools began to feel uncomfortable. Muraoka looked fidgety too. The next restaurant Toshio had in mind was closing when they approached, but reopened its doors to let them in. To drink. Toshio did not think he had a bottle there anymore, but the hostess found one with his name on it. Toshio could hardly recognize the writing. The men sat drinking in a small room. The hostess left them pretty much to themselves. The two men drank heavily, going long intervals without speaking.

Eventually Toshio felt that he needed something to eat. It was past midnight, they had yet to eat. Strange as it was, Toshio felt like he wanted to eat *takoyaki,* fried batter balls with octopus cut up inside. "Something to eat?" he asked.

"Even *ramen,*" Muraoka said. Steamed noodles in soup. A step up from *takoyaki* to be sure, but not that big a step. Perhaps Muraoka was not so bad.

"*Ramen* it is," Toshio said. There were shops every-where. Toshio knew one that used to be good and they sat down at a table inside. A young man worked there, clearly

127

too old to be a student. He took their order and began to prepare the food. Toshio watched the steam come up into his face, beading on his oily skin and dirty hair. Toshio fixated for a moment. No lifetime employment for him, he thought, no subsidized loans. No expense account. No retirement bonus. Just hourly work. As much as the boy wanted.

The young man served the *ramen*. "What are those newspapers for?" he asked.

"My son plays baseball," Toshio said and opened the paper. He tried to explain, tried to make a joke about it, but the boy misunderstood. The boy told another customer that Toshio's son had been a little league all-star.

"An all-star?" the man said. "Did he play in the Little League World Series?" He insisted on buying Toshio and Muraoka a beer.

Toshio felt ashamed. Of his liberties. Of himself. He felt ashamed of the *pachinko,* the *takoyaki*. Of his own inclination for the lowest level. He was ashamed that he had been showing what could at most be a mislabeled photograph. There were consequences, he knew, in a country so small that every inch was accounted for. Where every thing, every behavior had its own prescribed place.

"I don't understand," the man said. "He is your son or isn't he?"

Drunk as he was, Toshio's mind searched out the refuge. The exception. The one area in Tokyo whose neighborhood maps would never list the residents. Where men went who were dead to their families, who had unconditionally broken all ties. Where men went who were lost to the system. It was an area where executions had formerly taken place on the Bridge of Tears, an area called Sanya. Toshio knew that he thought about this area more than he should, felt a longing for the anonymity these men felt, understood the independence that alcohol granted them.

128

Toshio and Muraoka finished, then exited to the street. Muraoka stopped a taxi, thanked Toshio and said good-bye. Toshio stumbled ahead, for a second unsure how to direct himself home. He struggled to fix his position. That way to the Imperial Palace, he thought. Home of the emperor. And that way, he turned and thought, the other way to Sanya. Opposite edges of a society that seemed most occupied otherwise with pushing toward the middle.

Toshio knew that he would never enter the Imperial Palace as he would never enter the life of Sanya. He was, like everyone else he knew, subject to the inescapable pressure that said to be the same. And so only in his own mind, and sometimes when drunk, was he able to balance the limitations with the ambitions and to do it in his own way. To go where others could not find him. In the Sanya of his mind Toshio called his penis the emperor.

Home now, Emperor. March!

SEVEN

Nozomi examined the angle at which Toshio held his head. It would be her first clue to the extent of his hangover. The second was whether he could put words together or communicated through single words or a series of grunts. She rarely needed the third, but experienced the breath test anyway. He would also undergo the fourth: how poorly he walked the line to the bathroom. Nozomi had been through this many times before. When Toshio came home drunk she led the detoxification program. It was a process she had developed over many years. And while she was always looking for ways to improve it, she was sure she had saved many morning meetings.

The plan was to force fluids and get him into the bath as soon as possible with cold water ready. If the threat of cold water did not begin to scare Toshio into sobriety, she was willing to shoot it at him from the shower or turn it into the bath itself. Fluids, usually water and tea, worked to prevent dehydration, the worst part of a hangover, she had once read. There was an art to waking him in the morning too. Unless it was a Sunday, in which case she felt merely annoyed and not called upon, she found that indulgence was poorly rewarded. A brief, hard shake followed by a ten-minute break was the start. Then a "no-nonsense soldier" attitude to get him going and remind him that the world would make no allowances for his condition. It seemed to work out better if he didn't have too much to eat. The worst thing was when he threw up his breakfast.

Nozomi turned the cold water against a Toshio who had removed all but his underwear and who was holding what looked like a sports newspaper. "Hideki's picture," he said. She put the paper aside. Toshio could be pretty ridiculous when he was drunk. The last time he had asked her to confirm that his penis had grown larger over the years. She had her own agenda. She picked up his shirt. Toshio had a habit of leaning with his left arm when he ate. Reliably he could be expected to drop food or sauce on his sleeve. The more tired he became the more he leaned. So if he had been eating or drinking at a number of places, the food and drink tended to spill up his arm. Sometimes Nozomi could tell this way where he had been. But tonight she could pick up only traces of whiskey and *ramen*. Possibly the trick had run its course.

First thing the next morning, Toshio felt good and was surprised he had actually been so drunk the night before. He looked at Nozomi. He had liked being around her more lately. Not so much talking with her or doing things with her but just being in her presence. Her eyes, the way she turned her head. He marveled that she had been able to retain such an innocence, that she was so gentle, so patient. "I feel close to you," he said. "I don't know why."

We'll see how long it lasts, she thought. "Aren't you going to the office?"

"Am I bothering you?"

"No, it's just that I'm expecting . . . I don't know."

"I'll go."

Walking to the station Toshio thought about Hideki and the two games his team had played so far. Toshio had attended the first, a game against mediocre competition, which Hideki's team had won by a score of 2-1, largely on the pitching ability of the one little league all-star and the fielding ability of the other who, while technically assigned to left field, seemed to be taking advantage of his own mobility—and the other fielders' hesitancy—to cover much of the playing field by himself. On one play Toshio noticed that this athlete was actually foul of the right field line when he caught a pop-up. On another play this left fielder charged in from the outfield himself in order to run down a base runner trying to advance from second to third. Toshio sat behind the dugout during the game, but other than receiving what he felt was one icy stare from Coach Shimazaki and a team sun visor from the Seiko Matsuda look-alike he had little contact. Hideki had not played.

The next game, which Toshio had been unable to attend, had gone by all accounts differently. Shimazaki had refused to employ his star hurler two games in a row without proper rest and the team lost a 21-17 decision in a contest that had to be stopped at the end of the fifth inning because of darkness. Hideki appeared once in this game as a pinch hitter and struck out on four pitches. His best friend Hiroshi had, however, much to their mutual excitement, knocked in three runs on an infield single and some sloppy fielding.

Toshio boarded the train. Baseball was certainly easier to think about than the office. Things were going well, but at times it felt like too much to manage the detail involved, not to mention the obligations. There were so many different things to consider. He thought about the last letter he received from Ted Krane. "Why not join the Sweet Wells team?" Krane had written. Toshio had no interest in hooking up with a foreign company. He wrote back and asked to see Sweet Wells' financial statements. There was too much going on as it was to get involved with something that could lead Diamond Advertising astray.

Toshio thought about the time he had wasted with Muraoka the night before. The man's character, Toshio shuddered. He hoped he would not have to spend time like that with him again. It was easy to see a man's character when he was drunk. Of course, Toshio thought, it was easy to see a man's character when he wasn't drunk too.

And as for the office itself: the salarymen kept looking to him for things they should be doing themselves. The new opportunity with the microwave oven, for example. The machine that threatened, preliminary research indicated, the ability of the homemaker to make her own decisions. He could understand that. Just the other day he had seen a robot on television that made coffee, tea and toast. Toshio could feel the threat himself—squeezing at his own role in the middle.

The train pulled forward. Toshio did not feel quite so well now. He thought about whether or not it would be a good idea to get something to eat later, but when he closed his eyes he fell asleep. He dreamt that he was in a restaurant with waiters who kept bringing him rice, but wouldn't bring him anything to go with it. He remembered that he was asking to speak with the manager when the train pulled into the station.

Toshio got off the train and stopped at a newsstand to buy five more copies of the sports paper to take to the office. In this later edition, however, the article was positioned differently and the accompanying photograph was missing. Toshio started toward the office, but then decided he really wasn't feeling so well. It would be better instead to take advantage of Saturday's in-betweenness, he thought. To take the day off. He could see that a bank was closed; some Saturdays were bank holidays now. He had avoided making a clear policy himself, allowing his own presence most Saturdays and the pressure of the group to keep everybody in line. But it was his prerogative, he told himself, if he didn't want to go in.

Toshio wandered past the off-track betting office and then over to the discount electronics stores where he spent a few minutes confirming prices and then ordered the new model large screen television he had been thinking about. If Hideki was going to be on television he wanted to see it clearly. That was enough. The store could deliver it that afternoon.

Toshio located a pay phone on the street to call Nozomi. He wanted to tell her about the television, but was afraid she would ask how much it cost. "I'll be home a little early," he said.

"That's fine."

Nozomi looked at the laundry she had just folded. There was a test she had not applied the night before—the "traces of perfume/semen incriminating evidence" test. If they were there she knew she could find them. But she had not looked. It was easier not to think about.

(Something that Marcia Sloan could never understand: how when she asked her female students or friends how they felt about their husbands or their prospective husbands playing around, they always seemed to draw a blank. To stare away or to stammer.)

Nozomi had been thinking about Marcia in different terms. Against the best intentions she had not found the time to study, had not watched the public television station's English instruction nor had she tuned to the radio programs. For that matter she had yet to buy the magazines. While she still liked the idea of being fluent in English and thought it was a worthwhile goal, she could not deny that she was already dreading each lesson. Several times she had thought about canceling. She didn't mind the money involved and she was sure she could find an adequate excuse, but the effort of making the call was enough in itself to scare her off. And she felt she would be letting Marcia down. She did not want to disappoint Marcia.

Marcia arrived late, charitably. "If there were an Olympic event in loading and unloading buses and trains," she said, "I'm sure the Japanese would win."

Nozomi brought out tea and cake. Marcia had two helpings. There was a phone call from a friend Nozomi had not spoken with in a while and who expressed an interest in the lessons when Nozomi told her what she was doing. Nozomi did not really cut this call too short, and talking about the arrangements with Marcia afterwards should the friend join in was good for another ten or fifteen minutes. Marcia asked Nozomi a question about how to tie the belt on a kimono. Nozomi showed her. The lesson was passing quickly.

"Did I tell you my theory about Japanese festivals and the telephone?" Marcia asked.

Nozomi nodded. If she was wrong, she could live with it. "You have so many ideas."

"Back home we say that ideas are cheap."

"Really," Nozomi said. "In Japan we say ideas are valuable."

"And treat them like public property," Marcia said. They sat through an uncomfortable moment. "Did you watch the English program?" Marcia asked finally.

"I'm sorry," Nozomi said. "I haven't even picked up the magazines yet. But I will."

"That's all right," Marcia said. "There's really no hurry."

"It's not all right," Nozomi said and looked down.

135

Marcia thought about what to discuss next. Filling out the lessons had become more difficult lately. "Someone told me there were once women sumo wrestlers. Is that true?"

"It's true," Nozomi said.

"Can I ask you something else?"

"Of course."

"I heard," Marcia said, "that some Japanese companies won't hire women for managerial positions because they say there aren't enough qualified candidates."

"How did you know that?" Nozomi asked.

"Because my father sends me articles from American newspapers."

"Do you think that's terrible?" Nozomi asked.

"I'll tell you," Marcia answered, "it must be nice sometimes. Don't get me wrong. I mean the lack of a struggle. You know what you're supposed to do, you know what you're supposed to say. You have such a sense of peace and security. You don't have to worry. You don't even have to speak with your husband, do you?"

Nozomi smiled.

Marcia looked at her watch. Their lesson was almost over—another hour down. "I'll let you do the talking next week," she said when they stood up.

Marcia waved from the gate. Although she had seen it many times before, a Japanese woman in Western dress standing barefoot in her home, it was still discordant to her.

Nozomi watched Marcia walk away, then stood looking out. She thought about snow flowers. Snow without clouds, spontaneous snowflakes on cold days, even in sunlight: condensing, crystallizing, taking shape in a context in which they didn't belong, evaporating. Like her own feelings now, out of place.

136

A neighborhood girl stood making a call from the pay phone on the corner. Nozomi noticed Toshio approaching up the street.

"How was your lesson?" he asked when he found her.

"Fine."

"What did you do?"

"Mostly we just talked."

"What did you talk about?"

"We talked about Japanese life," she said, "what it's like and all the changes."

"That's great," he said. "I'll bet you'll never guess what I did this morning."

"What did you do?"

"I bought a new television set."

"Why did you do that?"

"Didn't you see Hideki's picture in the paper?" he asked.

"Which paper?"

"The papers I brought home with me last night."

She had placed them in the pile she kept for recycling by the back door. "I'll look," she said. "Where's the television?"

"They're going to deliver it," he said.

"When?"

"This afternoon."

"This afternoon?" she asked. "Why didn't you tell me?"

"I'm telling you now."

She took a deep breath. "I want to talk to you about something."

"Can it wait?" he asked. "I have a question for you. Something I've been working on."

She looked at him. "What?"

"Why don't you use a microwave oven?" he asked.

She knew why he was asking. So now he was selling microwave ovens. There it was again. The quiet, unending invasion of her household. And the split. Isolated, she knew, her side was defecting. One by one. "Food that's cooked in a microwave doesn't taste as good," she said. "It's heated differently."

Toshio looked at her disapprovingly. "Nozomi," he said, "they've tested that for a long time now and never found any proof that food cooked properly with a microwave oven tastes differently than food prepared by other means."

The doorbell rang. They looked at each other. "I'll get it," Nozomi said.

Just as well, Toshio thought. He knew how his agency should present it. With commercials that played on the intelligence of the housewife. That the modern housewife was at ease in today's world. That she used a microwave oven as an expression of her competence. Forget about taste, convenience or price. This would strictly be a matter of cultural ability. Flexibility. He felt confident. This was what he was paid for. It had been a productive morning after all.

Akiko waited for Nozomi at the door. Akiko had stopped by to pick up the videotape of her sister's wedding and was carrying some photographs of a recent weekend that her husband Massaki, their two children and she had taken to travel south to see the first cherry blossoms. Nozomi looked at the pictures. It was certainly not a good-looking family. From almost no angle could she say there was a pretty face, or was there a really good shot. But they did look happy. They had that shine. A feeling they were together. "You make me jealous," Nozomi said.

Akiko did not know how to respond. "No," she said and swallowed.

The phone rang. Toshio was in the other room, but Nozomi knew he wouldn't get up to get it. "Excuse me," she said to Akiko and moved to take the call.

138

It was Reiko, hysterical. "Hold on a second, Reiko," Nozomi said, "I'll be right back." She went out to Akiko. "This may take a minute."

"That's all right," Akiko said. "I can't stay long anyway." Akiko put her hand over her mouth. "I have an appointment with the doctor. Nozomi, I may be pregnant."

"That's wonderful," Nozomi said. "Are you pretty sure?"

Akiko held up four fingers.

"Four months, and you didn't go to the doctor?" Nozomi asked.

"I didn't want to jinx it," Akiko said. "We've been doing it so often, we were afraid we couldn't have another child."

"Let me know how it turns out," Nozomi said, "please."

"I will." Akiko turned to leave. "Thank you."

Nozomi rushed back to the phone. "I'm here."

"I have to talk with someone," Reiko said. "Nozomi, you're the only one I trust. Don't ask me what happened," she started crying into the phone. "Don't ask."

"Where are you, Reiko?" Nozomi asked.

"The coffee shop," she said. Then after a long pause, "The coffee boy."

"It couldn't be that bad, Reiko."

"I don't know what I'm doing."

"Well, if it's that bad," Nozomi said, "change coffee companies. You don't have to deal with someone you don't want to."

"I don't want to change coffee companies," Reiko said. The television delivery men knocked and called from the door.

"I'm sorry, Reiko," Nozomi said, "hold on." Nozomi went into the other room and found Toshio asleep with his head on the table. She woke him. "I have a call from Reiko I have to take. Do you think you could supervise the men with the television?"

"Do you have to talk with Reiko now?" Toshio asked.

"Yes, I do."

She went back to the phone, but no one was there. Only voices in the background. "Reiko?"

Footsteps, then Reiko's voice. "I can't talk," she said in a remarkably sobered voice. "Can you believe it? He's here now. I'm such a fool. I'll talk with you later. Thank you, Nozomi." She hung up.

Who was the fool? Nozomi thought.

The men had the television set installed in no time. The picture was good, but in the scale of the room it was all wrong. Overwhelming. It towered over everything. The men had Toshio turn through the channels to check the reception. He picked up a weather report. "Clear skies and cooler," the weatherman said.

Toshio looked outside. Right for once, he thought. He looked at the television again. The sky on the television set looked almost better than the sky in the window.

They turned to another station that was showing an around-the-town feature comparing the imitation food displayed outside of restaurants with the food actually served inside. The show focused on the biggest discrepancies. The men from the store both laughed. "The shrimp," one said. "Try the zoom."

"The steak," the other man said.

The educational channel featured a documentary outlining Japanese attempts to find oil, new overtures that were being made to drill in the South China Sea. "Let's look at something else," Toshio said.

Another station provided live coverage of a relay race held that day through the streets of Kyoto, the participating teams made up of junior high school girls. Streets had been closed off through the city in coordinated fashion to make the race possible. The picture looked a little better in the room. True, it took some getting used to, it was so commanding. But then a lot of good things took getting used to.

They turned to a professional baseball game. Toshio was feeling more and more vindicated. The game was of no interest, but the action on the screen was great, so close. Even the commercials looked better.

Toshio tuned next to a variety show where a young singer was finishing her number. Her arm movements and dance routine looked like they had been inspired by an airport ground crew guiding an airplane into its hanger. This is what Aihara had been pushing for. Production. With Hideo Ota's help, Aihara said that Diamond Advertising could develop its own talent. Starting with Yuko. He claimed that the firm could make her a star.

Toshio was skeptical. No question there was something appealing about the girl. Against his every expectation that the Yamaura people would reject the pictures for the cigarette lighter, they had insisted on using them. The office would almost certainly be asked to work on the breath freshener/cigarette lighter combination set planned for introduction later in the year. Toshio knew that an exclusive promotional contract with Yuko would not be that expensive. And he could certainly absorb the battery of singing and dancing lessons she would have to have. Toshio could lock her up; he did like that idea. Her career would be dependent on him. Let Aihara dream about developing the rest of the stable. Olympic athletes. Sumo stars. If anywhere, Toshio thought, the place to start was with Yuko.

The TV men returned to their truck. Toshio poured himself a beer. He was feeling better now. The world was looking good. He turned toward the picture. "No distortion," he said.

*

For Nozomi it was better to leave Toshio alone at moments like these. As it was, she had plenty on her own mind. The problem was that she had no experience. Nothing to draw on in circumstances outside of the home, nothing to call on in situations where she could not rely upon expected behaviors. She was awkward in the world outside of certain bounds, but at the same time she felt those boundaries drawing in. What's more, she now knew, something had moved inside her. Something had shifted, but with nothing to hold, guide or mold the change.

It was important to move outward. Not only for herself. She knew she was right. The world was changing. One day there would even be a woman prime minister. Why couldn't it happen? Legends depicted the origins of Japan as a matriarchy. It was the thoughts of being out in public that were so difficult. Like so many people, she thought she could begin. But she could not finish. Could not imagine.

She thought about the English magazines sold at the newsstand. She knew she should buy them. She had made the commitment. She did want to learn English and this was part of it.

As she walked quietly from the house she passed Toshio asleep in front of the television.

The lady at the kiosk asked if the magazines were for her children.

Her instincts were to say yes. But, "For me," Nozomi said. "I'm studying English conversation." For a second she had the hint of a feeling she had known about herself once before, but she couldn't hold it—it passed.

"Conversation is difficult," the woman said. "Everybody says so."

"Conversation is difficult," Nozomi agreed. She walked back to the house eager to open the magazines and set up a schedule.

Unfortunately, the magazines did not look so great back at the house. The course seemed too easy to be of practical value at first, but then where there were fine points or matters she didn't understand, the magazines were not enough.

"Nozomi," Toshio called, "something to eat!"

Lunch could wait for a minute. She had something she wanted to discuss. It was just an idea, but she liked the idea. Several hours a day. Not for the money, but to get out. For the experience. Somewhere was the right situation, the right job.

"That's a terrible idea," Toshio said. The idea of his wife working like that was embarrassing. "What about the children? Are you going to get up at four to take care of things here?"

Don't tell me how to raise my children, she thought. "Whatever it takes," she said, "I'll manage."

"Well, I'm hungry," he said. "Start there if you want a job."

"I think it would be better for us."

"I have everything I want," Toshio said. "If you need to get away, go to a hot springs for a few days."

"Your suggestion is distasteful."

"That's not what I meant," he said. Hot springs had earned a reputation as a place women went in search of affairs.

Nozomi went into the kitchen. She took a bowl of rice out of the rice maker and placed a red *umeboshi* plum in the center. It made what had once been called the national flag box lunch. White with a red dot in the middle. Like the flag; like a breast. The standard lunch in the days after the war when there had been no choices as to how to spend time or money. An experience so traumatic, so deep and widespread that it had become the uniform foundation upon which the nation was rebuilt. A country where people could walk at night without fear. A nation that led the world in automotive technology, but which provided subways and trains for its citizens. Clean trains, well-kept subways that ran on schedule. Well-equipped schools and pre-schools. Community organization. An industrial society that protected its farmers. She thought about the road her country was walking now. Of the drift.

She carried the lunch out and set it on the table. Toshio was watching a Coca-Cola commercial on the television. The Americans were wising up. This time the group was running around all together, singing, dancing and drinking Coke. Toshio knew what they were doing. He looked at his lunch. "Is this a joke?" he asked.

"What kind of joke?" she asked. The TV looked grotesque in the room. She turned toward her husband, but found her attention tracing back instead to the countryside where she had grown up, back to the stories she had overheard her parents tell when they thought that she was sleeping. The stories she had seen in the lines on their faces. Wasn't it easier, she thought, to remember those times with their sense of purpose than to confront what she was facing now? Shifting, forming, moving—then disappearing again. Like snow flowers on bright winter days.

To nothing.

EIGHT

Nozomi closed the door and stepped out of the house. "Steady" had been the word lately. Regardless of what might be going on around her—Toshio's preoccupation with what seemed like everything unrelated to their marriage, Hideki's transformation into his father, even Sanae's wavering allegiance. Regardless of the changes and the confusion, "steady" was the word.

Nozomi walked toward Reiko's coffee shop. It was not an appointment she had been looking forward to; twice she postponed. And then how glad she was to be going. To talk. She needed to be understood.

Crossing the street about a block from the house, Nozomi noticed a kitten lying in the gutter. It was a tiny gray kitten, emaciated, but still breathing. Nozomi looked, but could see no sign that this kitten belonged to anyone or was being taken care of in any way. Her impulse was to keep walking—to avoid the trouble and responsibility. But then, as if Sanae were watching her, Nozomi knew that this was not an adequate response. She placed the kitten in a cardboard box she found nearby and walked back to the house. Unfortunately they had run out of milk. She put the box on the back porch and walked out again. She could buy milk on the way home.

Nozomi found Reiko's cafe bar, less than five minutes late. Reiko should have been there. Somebody should have been there. Nozomi walked in and out a few times. Each time she entered a voice on the automatic door said, *"Irasshaimase."* Each time she walked out the voice said, *"Arigato gozaimashita."*

"Irasshaimase."

"Arigato gozaimashita."

"Irasshaimase."

"Arigato gozaimashita."

Nozomi looked around. What had Reiko been doing? The place was brand new, but already it looked like it was starting out in the wrong way. Outside lettering on the windows to announce the menu and prices had been put up poorly and was missing zeroes. Inside, so many of the chairs and tables were being used to hold Reiko's things that only two tables were completely empty. "Reiko?" Nozomi called.

There was no answer. Nozomi took a seat, but that felt unnatural. She stood up and started to clear one of the tables.

"Irasshaimase," the door opened. A young girl appeared. She seemed embarrassed to see Nozomi straightening up.

"Excuse me," she said and went directly to the back.

Nozomi didn't know what to do.

"Can I get you something?" the girl came out finally and asked.

"No, thank you," Nozomi said. "I'm a friend of Reiko's."

"Oh," the girl said, "well, just tell me if I can get you anything."

"Thank you," Nozomi said.

"Irasshaimase," the door opened again after a few minutes had passed—Reiko. She was carrying a bag of groceries.

"What do you think?" Reiko asked. "Do you like it?"

"*Arigato gozaimashita,*" the door closed in her face.

"*Irasshaimase,*" it opened again.

"I have to get that fixed," Reiko said. "What do you think? I couldn't decide whether to get it or not. Katsuichiro told me to go ahead. Do you like it?"

Nozomi didn't. Who puts a talking door on their own place? She felt embarrassed for Reiko. "Let me help you," she said, putting down the cloth she was holding and moving for Reiko's bag of groceries.

"You don't have to do that, Nozomi," Reiko said. "I have help now in the afternoons. Harue!"

The girl appeared from the back.

"Where's the gray skirt I asked you to wear?"

"I'm sorry," she said. "I took it to the cleaners."

"Oh," Reiko said, "well, I guess we'll have to get you another one, won't we? Where's my list?" She looked at the papers sitting by the pay phone on the counter. "Here," she said, handing Harue the groceries, "take this and get things prepped. Then come out and straighten up. The place looks terrible." Harue went back into the kitchen. "Sit down," Reiko said to Nozomi. "What would you like?"

"You don't have to get me anything, Reiko," Nozomi said. "These are for you." She handed Reiko two good luck charms she had bought recently at a temple and been saving.

"Thank you," Reiko said and squeezed Nozomi's hand, "but have something, okay? Look at the menu. Tell me what looks good." She handed Nozomi a menu.

Nozomi looked it over. Frankly, it all looked bad. "Maybe a glass of juice would be nice," Nozomi said.

"Harue!" Reiko clapped her hands. "One orange juice, please." She turned to Nozomi, "You know it's a lot more work than I had expected."

147

Nozomi nodded. She noticed the lines etched around Reiko's mouth from having forced too many smiles. Why had Reiko cut her hair so short?

Harue popped out from the back after a minute. "We must be out," she said. "I can't find any."

"How can we be out?" Reiko asked. "We don't have any customers."

"I'm sorry," Harue said. "Do you want me to check again?"

Reiko ignored her. "Have a cake set," she said to Nozomi. "Or the pilaf is nice."

Nozomi spotted an open bag of sliced carrots sitting on the counter. She did not really want cake set, but the thought of Reiko or this girl cooking. . . ."Cake and coffee would be fine," she said.

Reiko followed Harue into the back. Nozomi could hear Reiko speaking to the girl for drinking the juice.

Reiko reemerged with a slice of cake and an individually brewed cup of coffee. "She worked at another place before," Reiko said, "so she should know what she's doing."

Nozomi took a sip of coffee and started with the cake.

Harue came out. "I'm sorry," she said. "I found some juice after all. Would you like a glass?"

"I think I'm fine," Nozomi said.

"Harue," Reiko said, "if you make a mistake like that and I'm not here, don't ask. Just bring it out to the customer."

Harue brought Nozomi a glass of orange juice. It was hardly what Nozomi had in mind with cake set, but she accepted.

"She wants to be a singer," Reiko whispered after Harue went back into the kitchen. They laughed. Reiko took a small notebook out of her purse. "Gray skirt," she wrote, then added a question mark. "I keep two lists. You can't believe how many things are involved with a place like this."

"I can believe it," Nozomi said. "Wait until you get busy."

"That's a good one," Reiko said, shaking her head. "You know my friend from the coffee company? You should hear what he says. It's not so easy."

"That bad?" Nozomi asked.

"Not good. But to tell you the truth," Reiko lowered her voice, "I'm not concerned with the money anymore."

"I don't understand," Nozomi said.

"Because of Katsuichiro," Reiko said, "I don't care if we lose money."

Nozomi was puzzled.

"You know what they say," Reiko continued, "that there are a lot of good women, but not so many good men? Well, it's true."

"But he put up the money," Nozomi said.

"So what if he put up the money? What does that mean? He told me that he thinks about me all the time too. I said, 'What are you thinking about me?' Let's not be naive, Nozomi. If he gave me this place, imagine what he's giving her. I don't care if he wants to go out and play every once in awhile, but he shouldn't bring it into the house. He talks about it now when he's drunk."

"I'm sorry," Nozomi said.

"Why should you be sorry? You know what I tell him? I tell him he's lying. When he talks about his girl I tell him he's lying. We argue about it. What a situation."

Nozomi moved to take Reiko's hand, but Reiko pulled away.

"Where would I go?" Reiko asked. "That's all I need right now, isn't it? To tell my mother I'm separating from Katsuichiro." She paused. "Let me tell you about my husband. I don't know how he gets up in the morning without someone telling him what to do. I don't know how he does anything."

149

"Irasshaimase," the door opened. Two middle-aged women appeared at the door. If they were thinking about having a cup of coffee, Reiko's glare must have driven them away.

"Arigato gozaimashita," the door closed again.

"Coffee is dead," Reiko said. "I made a mistake. The market today is kids. I'm thinking I may have to get one of those ice machines."

Nozomi thought about Reiko working with kids. She was already in the wrong business. To think about Reiko working with kids was ridiculous.

Reiko took a deep breath. "Sometimes you think you can do anything you want," her voice trailed off. "I'm boring you. I know it. Tell me what's new with you."

Why get into it? Nozomi thought. Husband-bashing was common, not what she needed. "Nothing special."

"You're lucky," Reiko said. "You have everything."

Nozomi stood up. "I'll come again," she said. "We can talk."

"Where are you going?" Reiko asked. "Why are you rushing?"

Nozomi took her wallet out of her purse.

Reiko looked at the money Nozomi had set down. "What are you doing?" she asked.

"It's a business, Reiko," Nozomi said.

"I wouldn't hear of it."

"But your prices are too low," Nozomi said. "At least let me pay for the juice. How can you make money?"

"Do you think my prices are too low?" Reiko asked. "I can't take your money. What's gotten into you?"

"Just for the juice," Nozomi said, and would have gladly paid, but Reiko wouldn't accept it. Free, Nozomi knew through experience—even among friends—was usually the most expensive.

Walking home Nozomi thought about the way she spent her time now. She had begun making slight changes in organization: cleaning every other day instead of every day, arranging for a delivery, not working quite so hard to compare prices, skipping lunch. Once or twice she had even arranged her day with little more in mind than to leave time for a nap. Nobody noticed. Nobody seemed to care.

Nozomi felt relieved to leave. While Reiko's desperation and irrationality did make her feel more confident and self-assured in one way, seeing Reiko like this also introduced an idea with which she was not so comfortable, an idea she didn't like: the thought that not everything in life will work out well. That not every ending is a happy ending.

Nozomi turned into a small grocery store to buy milk. Somehow, she sensed, forces were conspiring to push her out from the center. While Sanae, Hideki and Toshio each had magnets pulling them irresistibly toward some destiny she knew they actually longed for, in her own life she was being left with the remainders. The corners that held no interest for the others. Ultimately the prospect of having little more opportunity than the continuing temptation to turn her unhappiness, unused time and surplus energy into the kind of general expression her mother-in-law was making. This was the revenge most often selected, Nozomi knew, by women who lived with the assumption that the lower a woman bows, the more she will be esteemed: make those women who are junior to you bow even lower. Then complain they aren't bowing low enough.

Turning onto her street Nozomi almost bumped into Akiko's husband, Masaaki. "So early," she said after collecting herself, "to be back."

"Akiko's pregnancy," he said. "Of course you know. I try to come home a little earlier to take the pressure off. We really appreciate your offer to help with Yukari. Akiko told me that there was no one in the world she felt more comfortable about leaving Yukari with than you." Masaaki was speaking to her directly, although his thick glasses altered eye contact.

"It's my pleasure," Nozomi said, "anytime."

"Thank you," he said.

The two stood without much to say. Nozomi felt that she should be more comfortable in this situation. What was the matter? She was speaking with her best friend's husband, that's all. Did she really have so little to say? She was acting so nervous. Embarrassed. As if she hardly ever spoke with a man.

Masaaki, she thought, was so warm. It was easy to see why Akiko felt for him. Even with his head tilted to the side, even with those glasses, he seemed able to look at her so directly. She felt her breath shortening, that she must be turning red.

"I'll tell Akiko I saw you," he said.

"Please," she said and turned away. She walked home quickly, but the incident was hard to dismiss.

Hideki was speaking on the telephone when she entered. "If a girl is uncomfortable being alone with you she'll bring a friend," he said into the phone, "but if she's comfortable with you she may bring a friend too. The best thing is to kind of ignore them."

"Where's your sister?" Nozomi asked.

"Upstairs," he said, "with some friends."

"What's she doing?"

"Mom, what am I," he asked, "a detective agency?"

She walked upstairs.

"Hi, Mom," Sanae said.

"What are you doing?" Nozomi asked.

"We're making Valentines," she said.

"Why are you doing that?"

"Because we want to. Are you mad because I took the glue out?"

"I'm not mad," Nozomi said. "It's just that Valentine's Day is not until next February."

"Well," Sanae said, "these are practice Valentines. Did you ever make one for Dad?"

The girls were looking at her. "We didn't really have a Valentine's Day when we were younger," Nozomi said. "It's new."

"What did you do then?" Sanae asked. She looked at her friends.

They laughed.

"I guess we didn't do anything," Nozomi said. "We didn't have a Valentine's Day."

The girls' attention turned back toward the cards they were making.

"Something to eat?" Nozomi asked.

"I'm not hungry, Mom," Sanae said.

"No?"

Sanae shook her head.

"Are you sure?"

The girls looked at each other. "Okay," Sanae said.

They started downstairs. "Mom?" Sanae asked.

"What is it, Sanae?"

"I just remembered something."

"What's that?"

"Dad called."

"What did he say?"

"He said that he wants you to call him."

"Anything else?"

"No."

They walked downstairs and into the kitchen. Hideki finished his conversation on the phone and then put on a funny-looking pair of glasses with the word "X-Ray" written on the side. "I can see through your dresses with these," he said to the girls who screamed and ran upstairs.

"Why do you do that?" Nozomi asked.

"Do what?" he asked.

"That," she pointed at the glasses.

"What?" he asked. "They don't care. In fact, I think they like it."

"That's not the point."

He put the glasses on and started looking over his mother.

"Don't start with me," she said.

"Don't you like it?" She moved to grab him. "Got to go," he yelled and ran out the back door. But he dropped his glasses on the way.

Nozomi picked them up. The glasses were nothing. What should she do with them? she wondered.

"Whoa!" Hideki came bursting into the house. "Who put the dead cat on the back porch? Sanae!" he screamed. "Sanae!"

Nozomi stopped Hideki in the middle of the room. She wasn't going to be sentimental about a dead cat, but neither was Hideki going to upset his sister. "That's enough," she said and walked him to the door. "Don't test me."

"What is it, Mom?" Sanae called from upstairs.

"Nothing," Nozomi answered. "I'll be up in a minute." She put the kitten in an empty plastic trash bag and then put the whole thing at the bottom of another almost-full trash bag.

Nozomi sat down in the kitchen. The remainders, she thought again about her prospects, the corners that hold no interest for the others. She looked at her magazines. What would it be like, she wondered, to arrange a meeting somewhere? Something safe, discreet, it didn't have to be often. There were ways for married women too.

154

What were her options? she wondered. There had been one period when she had used the flexible shower's head and spray to massage herself; there was another when she'd been able to reach orgasm simply by lying down and squeezing her legs together. It was hardly what she wanted. And what temporary release she did experience seemed only to intensify her deeper underlying dissatisfaction.

The phone rang.

"Do you think I'm being unreasonable," her mother-in-law asked, "to not want a new telephone number with so many fours in it?" "Four" shared a same pronunciation with the word "death."

"Couldn't Kazuo help you?" Nozomi asked.

"He's trying," she said. "I wish Toshio would show an interest from time to time."

"What would happen if you took the new number?" Nozomi asked.

"What?"

Nozomi repeated herself.

"How's Hideki?" her mother-in-law asked.

"Fine."

"Baseball," she said. "You kids are something."

Nozomi did not respond.

"Is everything all right?" her mother-in-law asked.

"Yes," Nozomi said.

"I didn't want to talk long anyway," she said. "I have to help your father-in-law get ready for a party he was invited to. Somebody who's retiring. Do you know what that man did? He worked as a ticket taker in a railway station. I don't know why your father-in-law even wants to go. The family is pretty nice though. I guess I'd be happy to be retiring too. Can you imagine that, working in a train station all your life?"

"Which station?" Nozomi asked.

"Nozomi," her mother-in-law said.

"Yes?"

"Please have Toshio call me when he has a chance."

"Why don't you call him at the office?" Nozomi asked. "I think he's there now."

"I don't like to bother him at the office. It interrupts him. You ask him to call me."

"When I see him," Nozomi said. They hung up.

Wasn't that the problem? Nozomi thought. That no matter how careful one was, no matter how discreet with the arrangements, someone else was bound to find out. Because someone was always watching. The wrong someone.

She went into the bathroom. There were drippings around the urinal. Men and women are different, she thought. Why should we be the ones to suffer for it?

Out of the corner of her eye she could see something moving on the floor. It was brown, relatively large, and for a second looked almost as if it had two heads. If it was an insect, she had never seen anything like it before. She took the handle of the sponge brush from its holder and moved closer. Heads in opposite directions, two of the biggest cockroaches she had ever seen were mating. She took the sponge brush and went after them. They broke up. She chased after one of them, but they ran back together. One ran across her foot. She beat them until they were dead.

She went into the kitchen and washed her hands. Then she sat down and picked up the phone. "I'm returning his call," she said to Mitsue.

"I think he's in conference, Mrs. Matsuzaka," Mitsue said. "Let me check."

"I can call back later," Nozomi said, but she was already on hold. That awful music came on. Couldn't they at least change the tape? she wondered. She had mentioned it to Toshio several times. Not that it was so important, but what

156

would clients think if every time they were put on hold—the same music?

"Nozomi?"

"Did you call before?"

"I called," Toshio said. "As a matter of fact, I called to see if you would pick up some blank videotapes for me."

"Oh," she said, "of course."

"Where were you before?"

"I went out."

"Where?"

"I went to Reiko's new coffee shop."

"Oh," he said, "I thought that maybe you had the snow-shoes on."

"What does that mean?"

"It means," he said, "that you are out looking for a job." He laughed.

Nozomi didn't answer.

"I'm kidding," he said. "Anyway, about the videotapes?"

"They're on my list," she said. "Don't worry."

"Don't forget."

"You don't have to remind me every two minutes about something like this."

"Just as long as you get them."

"Don't worry," she said.

They hung up.

He could get them himself.

She went upstairs to check on Sanae. "How about that snack we were talking about?"

Sanae looked at her friends. "Do we have to?"

Nozomi went downstairs and sat at the kitchen table. Sometimes when sitting she put her legs together because it felt good, but sometimes when sitting she crossed her legs to shut out the world.

The kimonos, she thought suddenly. Upstairs. For an instant she felt like taking them out and doing something to them.

No, she thought, don't do it—don't even think about it.

NINE

Toshio kept a stack of business-related books and periodicals on his desk. Self-improvement. Organization. Success. How to be a better salesman. How to be a more effective manager. Even inspirational stories about samurai businessmen opening new markets for their companies in Latin America and Africa. Toshio rarely read a book from cover to cover, preferring instead to scan indexes for a clue as to where to begin, or just allowing serendipity to choose today's two- or three-page selection. He liked to work a book this way for several weeks before placing it on his bookshelf with the others.

Toshio had thought it might be a good idea sometime to write his own book. A straight-talking, no-holds-barred dissertation on how to get ahead. Forget about the importance of teamwork or even the more recently fashionable approach, which stressed individual human development as well. The object of business was to make money. Toshio thought he could write in a first-person, friendly, chitchat style with lots of examples to illustrate what he was saying. The first case study, he imagined, would involve a chair and sofa in a reception area, which had become the center of social life in one office. By removing only the chair, Toshio would show it was possible for the manager to cut down on unnecessary conversation and improve productivity. Toshio would, through the course of his book, encourage readers to fraternize with office colleagues and employees *after-hours* not only to promote good feelings, but also to know what they were thinking—to be ready. Toshio would suggest that no manager had ever failed for seeming to be too friendly. He thought that his book could become important reading material for the widespread, though still often under-estimated technique of executive pretending, which he called "The Son-of-a-Bitch Management Method."

Toshio took out his *azuki* bean trading chart and wondered how the market had closed. He thought about calling his broker.

"Tatsu Taguchi," Mitsue called over the intercom.

Toshio picked up the phone. "Mr. Taguchi, how are you?"

"I'm fine, thank you. Yourself?"

"Thanks to you and everyone else," Toshio said. Tatsu Taguchi was a new client with a small Western-style restaurant chain. Taguchi had conducted his advertising in the past through a larger agency, but had called Diamond Advertising just the week before to discuss transferring his account on rumors now circulating that Big Catch Sushi's business was up twenty percent since what Toshio had thought was the bad publicity break. At least in the past it would have been a bad break. Anything controversial. Now it seemed as if people actually liked it.

"I studied the suggestions and media schedule your men put together," Taguchi said. "To be honest, I'm not sure."

Neither am I, Toshio thought. There was not the same need anymore, he reminded himself, to accept every account that walked in the door. The phone had been ringing, things were taking off. It was his opportunity to be more selective, more patient.

"How can I add a ten percent service charge to each check," Taguchi asked, "if I'm not going to give it to the help? How could I look my customers in the eye?"

"You wouldn't be the first," Toshio said, "believe me."

"And regarding these television spots," Taguchi said, "to be honest, I think we can do much better."

"To be honest myself," Toshio said, "there weren't many options available based on the budget you proposed."

"I understand," Taguchi said, "and as I told you, when we see the results we can increase the budget."

"Excuse me," Toshio said, "I want to look at your file." He put Taguchi on hold and pressed the intercom. "Mitsue, the Flamingo Restaurants folder, please."

He took a deep breath. Tatsu Taguchi. Takashi Muraoka of Maruichi Bank. There seemed to be more of these guys around lately. Toshio knew what to deliver on his end: "secret," "balanced," "family," "natural," "value," "quality," "famous," "respected," "new." That wasn't so difficult. But when it came time to get a real commitment, these new guys were nowhere. They wavered. They wasted so much time.

Mitsue placed the folder on his desk. The men had proposed booking the Flamingo chain on the televised swimming lessons—opposite a popular late-night variety show. He picked up the phone, "An audience of older men," he said, "who like to watch young people following instructions. We've had good luck here before. Do you want me to change it?"

"I don't know," Taguchi said. "What do you think?"

"Let's monitor the results," Toshio said. "I've been in this business for a long time and I can assure you, if we don't

160

achieve what we're looking for here we can always try something else."

Taguchi did not put up much more resistance before closing the conversation.

Some people just have to complain with their money, Toshio thought. He should have listened to Nozomi. She had never been willing to eat at a Flamingo Restaurant.

Tahara walked in.

"What is it, Tahara?" Toshio asked. He'd had considerably less patience with this junior salaryman since Yuko's dress-on-fire incident. The more he thought about it the less he liked the way Tahara had acted that day.

Tahara was carrying the shampoo bottle. "I'm sorry to disturb you with this," he said, "but the men thought that we should do something more than just change the directions for use. They thought it would be a difficult presentation to make to the client with just a change in the written instructions."

Toshio closed his eyes. As much as he felt like throwing Tahara out of the room, he realized that what he had just said was right. "Let me see it."

Tahara handed him the bottle.

"Have you used this shampoo?" Toshio asked.

"Once," Tahara said.

"And?"

Tahara shrugged.

"The usual, I assume."

Tahara nodded.

"Let's add some writing in English," Toshio said. "Something in big letters across the front. Something we can pick up later."

"Something sexy," Tahara said.

"That's right," Toshio said, "something sexy. You make it up."

"I'll work on it."

"Good," Toshio said, pausing to think for a second. "Let's change the color too."

"Blue?" Tahara asked. He had read a study suggesting people preferred soap products packaged in blue.

"No," Toshio said, "yellow." He read those surveys too. People answer blue and then they buy yellow. "What else?"

"A man came in the other day," Tahara said. "We thought we should show you."

"Show me what?"

"I'll get it." Tahara ran out of the room and came back with a box he quickly unpacked. "It's an ice cream maker," he said, "for the house. Do you want to see how it works?"

Toshio remembered the day Tahara had come into his office with a phonograph record and what looked like a toy car. Tahara had placed the record down flat in the center of his desk and put the car on top of it. The car raced around and around the record playing music. Tahara had clapped a few times, a big grin on his face. But he had just been a rookie then. Toshio looked at Tahara who was explaining that the ice cream maker played a jingle automatically at key points to indicate where the machine was in its cycle. Toshio could see how hard Tahara was trying, the extent to which he was going out of his way to ingratiate himself again after realizing his obvious blunder and perceived defection during the dress-on-fire aftermath. Tahara clapped a few times to the ice cream maker's jingle. Toshio actually felt a little sorry now, realized the strain Tahara was under. But it wasn't enough for Toshio to change his demeanor. They were going to be together for a long time; there would be plenty of opportunities to work things out. Tahara may have been clapping, but Toshio did not feel like dancing.

"What do you think?" Tahara asked. "It's a novelty item. Do you like it?"

162

"I like it, Tahara," Toshio said. "I like it all."

"Do you think we can do something with it?"

"Tahara," Toshio said, "some products don't need advertising."

Tahara understood. He began to pack the machine.

"Do we have to return it by a certain date?" Toshio asked.

"No," Tahara said, "in fact, we don't have to return it at all. It's ours to keep."

"Good," Toshio said. "Leave it here." Just because he wasn't interested in advertising it didn't mean that the ice cream maker would not make a nice gift. "What else is on your mind?"

"I spoke with Aihara this morning," Tahara said, "from the studio. He said that he and Hideo Ota had selected a first song for Miss Tanioka. If that's all right."

Toshio looked at Tahara. Didn't he know the raw nerve he was working here? "She just started with the singing lessons two weeks ago, and we're ready to release a single nationwide?"

Tahara smiled sheepishly. "It really doesn't take that long, does it?"

"I don't know," Toshio said. "What's the song called?"

"'Dreamy, Thinking of You,'" Tahara said.

"'Dreamy, Thinking of You'?" Toshio asked.

"'Dreamy, Thinking of You,'" Tahara confirmed.

"Have you heard it?"

"No, but if we don't take it someone else might."

Toshio nodded and tapped on his desk a few times. He looked at the Flamingo Restaurants folder, the shampoo bottle, the ice cream maker, his golf clubs in the corner, the books and the *azuki* bean chart draped over the suburbs of his desk. "Those numbers Aihara put together," Toshio asked, "do you think they're realistic?"

"As far as I know," Tahara said.

Miho walked in with some filing. "I'm sorry," she said, "have you seen the Flamingo Restaurants folder? One of the men is looking for it."

"Here," Toshio said. He closed the folder and handed it to her. She was certainly beautiful.

"Thank you," Miho said and began to put some things away in his filing cabinet. Toshio trailed her with his eyes. How practical would it be, he wondered, to change the office seating arrangement in the bull pen so he could see her more clearly from his desk?

"Sir?" Tahara asked.

"It's too soon, Tahara," Toshio said. "This is still a business, remember?"

"And if someone else takes the song?"

"We can berate ourselves later."

"Understood," Tahara said. His disappointment was obvious.

"But there is one thing you can do for me," Toshio said.

"Yes?"

"I'd like to see our prospective 'talento' again in my office one day before she becomes a star. Do you think that could be arranged?"

"Of course."

"Thank you, Tahara."

"Thank you, sir." Tahara backed towards the door.

Toshio folded his *azuki* bean chart and looked at the papers on his desk. The mail. The messages. She was still at the filing cabinet; it was hard to concentrate. "'Dreamy, Thinking of You,' Miho. What do you think?"

"What?"

"I mean as a song title." He laughed. "You know we're thinking about getting into production around here."

"That's nice."

164

Beautiful. He didn't know what to say. She was beautiful, but he couldn't hold a conversation with her. They always dead-ended. "You know, Miho, you actually look a little Chinese."

"Do I?" she said and walked out.

Forget about her, Toshio thought. He pulled out the desk drawer where he had taped the picture of Hideki from the sports paper inside. He enjoyed looking at it. Even if he knew it was a mistake, Toshio was pleased that Hideki was in a position where this kind of thing could even occur. And Hideki looked good, there was no mistake about that.

Toshio had still not decided whether to go to the game, but was leaning toward watching it on the new television set at home. The six hours required for the round-trip on the train to Osaka coupled with the shellacking he was likely to have to endure in the sun—with Hideki almost certainly on the bench the whole time—directed Toshio's thoughts toward the air conditioning and beer available at home. That way he could also monitor the videotaping himself. Even when they set the timer in advance Nozomi made mistakes with the machine.

Toshio felt the pressure of another issue working here as well. Something about which he would have preferred not to think, but which he could not avoid. Because Hideki had been acting as if Toshio's participation, even limited to going to the games, was somehow a threat to his own interests. A violation of his territory and a hindrance to his efforts to succeed. Toshio had tried to discuss it with him once, and Hideki had not cooperated.

Hideki was now batting 1 for 5 on the season. In the two games Toshio had attended Hideki had not played in one and had grounded out to the pitcher in the other. His one success on the season was a towering home run Toshio had not seen, but which had apparently inspired Coach Shimazaki to call Hideki his team's "secret weapon."

Tahara walked in. "All set," he said. "We've scheduled a meeting with Miss Tanioka. I told Mitsue."

"Good," Toshio said. "And did you tell Aihara we have to pass on that song?"

"I tried," Tahara said, "but I couldn't reach him. They said he was on his way back from the studio."

"Ken Kondo on line two," Mitsue buzzed.

"Excuse me," Toshio said to Tahara, waving him out of the room, "but don't forget."

"*Moshi, moshi,*" Kondo said over the conference box. His voice was hoarse.

"*Moshi, moshi,*" Toshio answered.

"*Moshi, moshi,*" Kondo repeated.

"*Moshi, moshi,*" Toshio replied. "Ken, what's wrong? You sound terrible."

"Business," Kondo said. "Let's face it, when it gets this busy you wonder if it's worth it."

"It's worth it," Toshio said. "What's happening?"

"I have to find a doctor to accompany the group I have going to the Philippines next week," Kondo said. "Too many complaints from the wives recently."

"Is it hard to find a doctor?" Toshio asked.

"No," Kondo said, "but they all want to get laid. I mean paid." They laughed.

"Problems with VD?" Toshio asked.

"Thank God," Kondo replied. "If that other stuff gets over here I'm finished."

"I understand," Toshio said.

"What's happening with you?" Kondo asked. "Any luck with your new star?"

Toshio took Kondo off the speaker box and onto his private line. That Kondo was like a heat-seeking missile. If there was anything there he could feel it. Toshio recognized a tinge of jealousy in his own reactions already; he felt protective, did not want to introduce Ken to Yuko. "We haven't broken any new ground," Toshio said. "Have a meeting in my office sometime next week, I think. You know, Ken, there are people who would kill for an opportunity like this."

"Including you," Kondo said. They laughed. "What else is going on? I've been so busy I'm afraid I'll lose track of you."

"Ditto on this end," Toshio said. "I have so many things to do, the list must be longer than my penis."

Kondo paused. "With an erection, I hope."

"Very funny," Toshio said.

"By the way," Kondo said, "I'm looking forward to this party you're having."

"I don't understand," Toshio jested. "The men were instructed to invite only the most important clients. How did you get an invitation?"

"There must have been a mistake," Kondo said.

"That's safe to assume around here."

"What should we do?"

"I'll let it go," Toshio said, "but just don't let me see you running around the room looking for business."

"I promise, but why should we wait until then? Any chance to get together this week?"

Mitsue walked in and handed Toshio a garbled fax. "I'd like to," Toshio said to Kondo. "What does your schedule look like?" He couldn't read the fax. "What is this?"

"What?" Kondo asked.

"I don't know," she said.

"Ken, I'm sorry," Toshio said, not feeling as comfortable with Mitsue in the room. "Let me call you later."

"Sure," Kondo said, "anytime."

Toshio hung up. "What is this, Mitsue?" The fax was written in English. "I can't understand one word of it. Are you sure it's for us?"

"I don't know. Tahara couldn't read it either."

"It's probably a mistake," Toshio said. "If it's important I'm sure whoever wrote it will contact us again."

He nodded to dismiss Mitsue before calling his broker.

"I'm sorry," the receptionist answered, "he's tied up on another line. Would you like to hold?"

"That's all right," Toshio said. "I'll call back later."

"Any message?"

"No message, thank you." He stood up. He felt restless. He walked out to Mitsue's desk. "Mitsue." He wanted to lecture her about interrupting him while he was on the phone, but he heard voices in the conference room. He looked at his watch. The afternoon meeting? It was not that time. "Who's in the conference room?"

"I don't know," she said. "Do you want me to look?"

Toshio shook his head no. He knew. A few of the men had assembled for the kind of spontaneous bull session that sometimes occurred during the lunch hour or when they went out drinking together at Applause, or on rarer occasions before work, or when something very exciting was happening during the workday itself. What had captured the interest of his men today? Toshio wondered while sauntering over. Dropping into these informal meetings, carefully, was an effective way to gauge what was happening in the office. Judging by the intensity of the discussion it must have been something big. Toshio paused outside the door.

"'Fashion Girl,'" he heard Tahara say.

"'Good Sweat Tonight,'" Shibata offered.

"'Beach Party Yo-Yo.'" Yamamoto said.

"But have we even decided to go ahead with this?" Toshio could recognize that voice anywhere: Mr. Worry Wart. Saeki himself.

168

Toshio stepped into the room. Into a give-and-take, round-table discussion of specific song titles to pursue should "Dreamy, Thinking of You" turn out to be a success. Tahara stood by the blackboard where the suggestions had been hastily scribbled. Toshio looked at the titles on the blackboard. "What are you doing?" he asked.

The men looked embarrassed. Only Yamamoto was perky now, apparently oblivious to the implications of the moment. "We're waiting for Aihara," he said, "right?"

Silence. Tahara squirmed by the blackboard. Shibata looked down and to the side. Toshio chose not to ease the tension by speaking himself, but during the ensuing silence he could not miss seeing that Saeki especially looked noticeably subdued, even depressed. As if Saeki had been defeated, he seemed so distressed. A mental note, Toshio thought, to speak with Saeki privately. Saeki should not be the one to suffer for this.

Aihara appeared at the conference room door—his arrival for the day. Aihara was carrying a good-looking leather briefcase and wearing what appeared to be a new pink shirt.

"Irasshaimase," Toshio said sarcastically. He felt like biting Aihara's head off. "Do you carry a watch, son?"

"Of course," Aihara said. He took a credit card-sized calculator/timepiece out of his back pocket. "It's 10:40."

The men tried not to laugh.

Newcomers work well for the first twenty days, Toshio recalled the saying. It looked like Aihara's time was up. Where were the twenty days?

"I'm sorry I'm late," Aihara said, moving to the front of the room, "but I think you'll understand. Sir," he asked Toshio, who was standing in the back, "would you close the door, please?"

The salarymen turned to watch Toshio close the door.

Aihara opened his briefcase. "Hideo Ota got the list of record stores they sample in putting the charts together," he said. "The Best 10. The Top 100. You know." He pulled out some papers. "It's pretty straightforward. If we cover

169

Tokyo and Yokohama thoroughly and buy out just a few, I'm not talking about that many, stores in Hokkaido and in the Northeast we affect what they think are the results from sixty-three percent of the nation's record stores."

He has a good sense of humor, Toshio thought.

"It's not complicated," Aihara continued, "When 'Dreamy, Thinking of You' is released we buy out the key locations and the record breaks into the charts. People see the record on the charts and they buy. Supportive marketing." He smiled. "We want to get into the charts."

Toshio felt a little dryness in his throat, a little wet under the armpits. He had worked long and hard to build Diamond Advertising into what it was. The men were looking his way. "How many stores are involved?" He knew he sounded meeker than he should.

"Forty-six," Aihara said. "Most of them in Tokyo. About another ten in Yokohama. Three in Sapporo. Five throughout the Northeast—four of those along the bullet train line that should be pretty easy to cover and then a little dandy they use to represent every town in the country with fewer than a thousand people. Look at this." He pulled out a map of the archipelago with key locations marked.

"What's the name of the town?" Toshio asked.

"Sakuramachi," Aihara said, "it takes about twelve hours to get to from Tokyo."

"Well, you can forget about that one," Toshio said, "but don't you think it looks a little strange that a first-time act has so much success in such specific areas?"

"That's why we schedule a couple of concerts," Aihara said, "so the record sales seem to be in response to her concerts."

"But she only has one song," Toshio said.

"We use other people's songs to fill out the concert," Aihara said. "In the meantime we're gearing up for the future."

170

Tahara raised his hand. The map was in front of him. "Sir," he spoke directly to Toshio, "you won't believe this, but if it's the same town, I actually have an aunt who lives there. I could call her and ask her to buy the records for us." He stood up.

"Where are you going?" Toshio asked.

"To call my aunt," he said, "to see if it's the same town."

Let him go, Toshio thought.

The men were looking his way again. While there was certainly a part of himself that would have liked to proceed with something different like this, the greater coalition was speaking louder. "Don't," it said. "Call Aihara into your office for redirection. Reestablish authority in the office and get back to business."

"There's another aspect to this," Aihara said. The men turned their attention his way again. "In addition to the charts, the weekly television shows choose their performers based on the number of postcards they receive from the general public. I've programmed the computer to do the addressing for us with return addresses proportional to the locations of the record stores we're buying out. But I think the face of the card should be written by hand so we don't arouse too much suspicion." Aihara took out a box of crayons and began to give a demonstration. "We put down her name and the name of the song, but it's better if it looks like it was written by a junior high school girl."

The men seemed to be impressed.

"I share your concern," Aihara said to Toshio, "about the costs involved and the time this will take, but we only have to do it in the beginning. After that the fans take over."

Aihara began writing numbers on the board. It was important, Toshio reminded himself, to develop a team capable of creative independence. He had been trying to do this for years.

171

Saeki raised his hand. "I'm sorry," he said. "This is not an area I have experience with, and it's certainly not the money, but I worry about doing something like this."

"I know what you're saying," Toshio said. And I worry about the money too.

Yamamoto, who was sitting within reach of Aihara's briefcase, held up a postcard he had just finished coloring. "Yuko Tanioka," the card said in different colors, "'Dreamy, Thinking of You.'"

That was enough. "I'll think about it, Aihara," Toshio said. It was all he needed, to have half his men running around the city in pairs buying copies of a record that he was paying to produce while the other half was coloring postcards.

"I think we should probably go ahead with this," Aihara said. "We went to some risk to get the list of record stores and they change it from time to time. The song is right. I won't tell you that Miss Tanioka is going to win any awards yet on the merits of her voice, but her image is good and that's what we need."

Tahara came bursting into the room. He was perspiring. "I called her," he said. "She wants to have the money first."

"Who?" Toshio asked.

"My aunt," Tahara said. "I didn't want to go into detail with her. She's a suspicious lady and she wants to have the money before doing anything."

"We can send it by mail," Toshio said, reacting.

"She was concerned about that," Tahara said. "She asked about what happens if the money's lost. She doesn't want the responsibility."

Toshio turned to his men. "Has anyone here ever had a problem sending cash in the mail?" He could feel the accumulated tension of having had to pilot his crew through so many tight situations welling up in his shoulders. "What

172

do I have to do, Tahara? Go up there and give it to her myself?" He took the money he was carrying, along with the other contents in his right pocket, and threw it all out on the table. Cash, a neatly pressed handkerchief, a set of keys, and a rubber. How did that get there?

The men laughed.

"I wish you would give it to her, sir," Tahara said.

The men laughed again.

Toshio looked at the chalkboard where Aihara was writing simple projections—marketing Yuko with the proposed strategy and marketing Yuko without. There was not much choice between the two. Toshio wondered if Aihara was aware of the true principle along which he was manipulating his boss: that at some point everybody's fantasies turn on the appearance of being forced to do what one really wants to do anyway.

A few of the suggested song titles remained written on the board beneath Aihara's projections. Yamamoto was pretty good with this, Toshio thought. When he tried to think of a few titles himself it seemed that the good ones had already been made into songs. What did he know about this kind of thing? "Pass," the voice in the back of his head said. "Pass."

"I'm sorry," Mitsue said, opening the door, "your wife is on the phone. I didn't know what to tell her."

Toshio turned to the men. "Rent the smallest concert hall you can find in Hokkaido." He would tell Yuko personally. "But move carefully. We're breaking new ground here." Diamond Productions, he thought. He hoped Aihara knew what he was doing. "Move carefully," he said, "but let's do it."

Let's do it, he thought. Do what you want.

TEN

"Nozomi!" Toshio called from the new television set. "Did you touch any of these dials?"

"No," she said. "Why?"

"Because I'm having a hard time getting the picture right." Toshio had decided to watch the game at home because—and he would not have said this to anyone—if his son was going to be on TV he wanted to watch him on TV. "Where's Sanae?"

"She's at a friend's," Nozomi said and went into the kitchen. She thought Toshio was saying something now from the other room, but she missed his words in her preoccupation. "Just a second," she said, lifting his lunch tray. She walked out to the living room. "Did you fix the picture?" she asked. Toshio had such a serious look on his face. "What's wrong?"

"Do you want to?" he asked. "What I was saying?"

"Do I want to what?"

"Didn't you hear me?"

"Did you say something? I couldn't hear you. What happened to the game?"

174

"The game doesn't start for another half hour," he replied. "What do you think? How many chances do we get on a Saturday afternoon? I'd like to."

"Oh," she said, "but I can't. My period." She put the tray down. "I'm sorry."

"Forget it."

Toshio turned his attention to the screen. The picture needed adjustment because the colors kept shading toward yellow and purple. Equally disconcerting was the ragged intrusion, which looked like an aggressive amoeba and which kept appearing on the left side of the screen. The problem seemed to be of varying intensity depending on the channel and playing with the dials helped to control it. Toshio was able to sharpen the picture and correct the colors, but he could only get it completely right on the wrong station now, and worse, after a few minutes the palette began to lean again. Working with the knobs seemed to help, but when he tried to adjust the hue control he found that its button was already turned completely to one side. The hue control wasn't working.

"We can bring the other set down," Nozomi suggested.

We can bring the other set down, Toshio mimicked her in his mind. "We'll have to."

"It doesn't matter which set we use as long as we watch," she said, "right?"

It matters to me, Toshio thought.

He brought the other set from upstairs and placed it on a small cart next to the oversized set, leaving both on for the time being. The broadcast was scheduled to begin at 1:08. Toshio tuned both sets to the channel that would carry Hideki's game. An economics professor from a leading university was suggesting that recent American moves to let the dollar go would ultimately result in another round of worldwide inflation. May it arrive in time to rescue my commodities position, Toshio thought. He was now long five contracts of *azuki* beans.

Nozomi did not like her husband's behavior, the gruffness with which he was acting. She stepped into the kitchen. At least there was some privacy in the kitchen. People might say it was a man's world, but she, for one, had no desire to trade places.

The broadcast began and the players from Hideki's team were introduced. Each wore a number assigned by order of height. The former little league all-star who played left field for Hideki's team wore number one—a real bear. Because he was the second tallest member of the team, Hideki wore number two. "Nozomi!" Toshio yelled. Hideki looked good. Aside from the question of whether he had any athletic ability, he certainly looked the part. Hiroshi wore number four. He looked good too. Shimazaki's little league pitcher wore number seven. Toshio had forgotten how small and thin he was. He would have never picked him out as the athlete he was supposed to be. This pitcher comported himself with such fine movements. Toshio could understand the mistake in the sports paper. Someone had probably obtained a team picture and cut off the two tallest members on the end. Toshio knew how these things worked.

Nozomi came out to see Coach Shimazaki step up from the dugout and wave to the crowd. Shimazaki was impeccably groomed and looked as if he had been pressed at the same time as his uniform. Even in baseball pajamas, even in the context of a high school game, Shimazaki looked right.

Toshio felt optimistic. "They showed Hideki."

"How did he look?" Nozomi asked.

"Scared." They laughed.

The camera lifted to pan the fans in the stadium where the rooting section was up and in full force. For an instant

Nozomi thought that she saw Hideki's girlfriend in front with the other cheerleaders and leading a cheer. "Hideki's girlfriend," she said.

"Where?" Toshio asked, but the camera moved so that the introductions could begin with the other team. "Hideki has a girlfriend?"

Seeing the athletes from the Osaka powerhouse was not encouraging. The way these players stood, the experience behind their smiles, the added confidence that says home team. Toshio guessed that Hideki would have worn only number five or six with this team. Toshio could also see that the Osaka coach was no slouch himself. The announcers mentioned several times the rivalry he and Shimazaki had enjoyed in their brief careers as pros, a rivalry that had supposedly focused on who was more effective at carrying out instructions. The Osaka coach came out of his dugout to acknowledge the crowd and then gave a brief salute to Coach Shimazaki who returned it with equal dignity. The Osaka team took the field.

The top of the first inning passed quickly. The Osaka pitcher struck out Shimazaki's shortstop—the captain and lead off batter—on three pitches. Then Hideki's team's own pitcher grounded out on a ball hit directly to the first baseman. Finally the Osaka pitcher fanned the all-star left fielder on five pitches, the last of which left him swinging so hard he looked like he might fall down. Toshio could see that the other pitcher wore number one. Toshio was afraid it would not be much of a game.

Despite his smaller size, however, Shimazaki's pitcher managed to hold his own. The kid worked slowly, taking long concentrated looks at the plate before throwing. Toshio thought that this pitcher looked more like he belonged in *juku* than on a baseball field, but he retired the other team

177

easily, facing four batters, the one reaching first on a throwing error by the third baseman.

Shimazaki's fielders returned to an enthusiastic greeting in their dugout. Coach Shimazaki remained cool, the camera recording a controlled, but challenging, smile that he now directed at the Osaka coach. Toshio felt more hopeful suddenly, almost excited. Unfortunately the invading amoeba was destroying the picture on the large screen and the set was beginning to make static too. Toshio turned it off; he thought about calling the shop, but was afraid a repairman would be sent to the house while the game was still on.

The second, third and fourth innings moved quickly, Hideki's team going down without much fight it seemed, except when the little league all-stars came up to bat, and then the team still went down. It just might have taken a little more time.

The announcers stressed how unlikely it was that first-year students, even little league all-stars, could make much of an impact against the more experienced Osaka team. "With such a weak supporting cast," one announcer said, "it's almost a two against nine situation for Shimazaki's club." The announcer recalled that the Osaka school had sent six players to the pros over the years and suggested that the team's ranks were swelled by several players with this same kind of ability. Osaka was undefeated at 15-0, having played several extra games en route to winning the national spring tournament, which had additionally given the team the advantage and experience of having played on national television. Hideki's team had entered the match with a more modest 5-3 record. "It should just be a matter of time before form prevails," the announcer said, "but it's a fascinating game to watch anyway. Shimazaki has always been a personal favorite. I would enjoy watching him coach at any level."

"Really to his credit," the other announcer said.

Save it, Toshio thought.

The phone rang.

"Our neighborhood *okonomiyaki* restaurant," Nozomi said afterward, "called to say they were watching."

"That's great," Toshio said, returning his attention to the game. He noticed that Shimazaki's pitcher seemed to be approaching the mound a little more slowly each inning. The Osaka team was making contact, fouling balls deep into corners, putting men on base, hurting Hideki's club. During the first several innings the response in Hideki's dugout had been almost unrestrained. Toshio now saw less enthusiasm, more a relief that time was passing and that there had been no accident rather than that their team was still involved in the game. Not that the other team's players looked so invincible. Toshio knew what frustration looked like. They were flexing big muscles when they warmed up with the bat, their pitcher was throwing hard and inside—several times he brushed back one of Shimazaki's players. Toshio knew it was unnecessary. The Osaka pitcher was trying to intimidate Shimazaki's squad because in some way he and his teammates had been intimidated as well.

In the bottom of the fifth inning Hideki's team managed to get out of a bases-loaded one-out situation when the left fielder made a magnificent catch of a dropping fly ball hit shallow to left field and then allowed his momentum to carry him across third base, achieving the last out because the base runner had mistakenly tried to score from third on batter's contact, so unlikely did it seem that the left fielder could catch the ball. There was a lot of territory out there, but a disproportionate amount of balls seemed to be going toward left. It was as if by the left fielder's personal concentration, or rather by a combination of his and the pitcher's and Coach Shimazaki's, that the other team was directing so many balls his way. At the end of the fifth inning the other team had six hits, but it was still a 0-0 tie. High school contests go seven innings. Perhaps it was already a victory, Toshio thought. Extra innings had not been imaginable.

The telephone rang: Reiko. She reported that Harue had not shown up. She said that she really appreciated Nozomi's stopping by the other day and it had made her think—would Nozomi reconsider her decision?

"Reiko," Nozomi interrupted, "Hideki's game is on television. Can we discuss this later?"

"Oh," Reiko said, "of course. I didn't realize. What channel?"

Coach Shimazaki pinch-hit Hiroshi in the top of the sixth inning and allowed him to stay in the game in right field. The left fielder seemed to be waving and counseling Hiroshi before nearly every defensive play on how to position himself. The other team, realizing Hiroshi's vulnerability, appeared to be making a bigger effort to hit that way, fouling more and more balls down the right field line. Hiroshi looked very nervous on the field—like he didn't belong.

A conference was called on the mound. The shortstop, pitcher, catcher and left fielder all came in to talk. Their faces were serious. Toshio could see the dirt and perspiration on their necks. There were no men on base, Toshio did not know why they were speaking. Then he noticed that the catcher had taken off his mitt and was massaging his palm. Shimazaki came out now from the dugout to join the conference. He examined the catcher's hand. The little pitcher may not have looked like he was throwing so hard, but he had put his catcher out of action. "A tough break for

Shimazaki," one of the announcers said. "His team had been doing pretty well until now."

"And a tough decision to make," the other announcer replied. "I don't see a back-up catcher listed on their roster."

Shimazaki stepped back while considering his next move. The other coach stood confidently looking out from his dugout with his arms folded. Shimazaki made his decision and began giving instructions. The catcher started taking off his equipment and handing it to the shortstop who then held it for the left fielder who began putting it on. Toshio thought he saw Hideki make a tentative move to put on his glove in the dugout, but then Shimazaki waved him away, was pointing more directly at another player.

"Why not Hideki?" Toshio said out loud.

"What's happening?" Nozomi came in from the kitchen. Toshio's anxiety level made her feel uncomfortable.

"Very nervous," Toshio said.

"Are we losing?" she asked.

"No, still tied."

"Really," she said. "Did you see Hideki?"

"In the dugout," he said. "He looks good."

Play resumed. Although at first cautious, the pitcher actually seemed to be able to open up a little more, to throw harder with his new catcher. The transformed left fielder did not seem to have the catcher's crouch down just right, did not seem to disguise his signals very well, and he seemed to be talking to himself, but the pitcher was firing and his catcher was catching. The field looked a lot smaller all of a sudden, even with Hiroshi in right. "Two outs," Toshio could read the catcher's lips. "Three outs." Out of another inning and into the top of the seventh.

"We're going to stay with the game until it's over," the announcer said, "even into extra innings."

181

Toshio could see Hideki speaking to Hiroshi in the dugout. Hiroshi looked ash-white, pale as a ghost.

"The pitching has been magnificent," one announcer said. "The Osaka hurler working toward what could be his sixth career no-hitter, having allowed only one walk the entire game, and Shimazaki's ace pitching an equally masterful, if slightly less perfect, game. Who would have expected to see the possibility of extra innings?"

The other announcer agreed. "Really a tribute to the level of the high school game today," he said, "to see two teams with two such fine coaches going at it like this."

Let's go, Toshio thought.

The seventh inning passed without major incident other than some rain clouds, which appeared on the horizon with an occasional gust of wind. The eighth inning passed uneventfully as well. Toshio thought that Hideki's pitcher was looking stronger now as the transformed left fielder seemed to be getting the hang of things behind the plate in his role as catcher. But the other team's pitcher looked good too.

In the top of the ninth inning the Osaka pitcher put two men down quickly before surrendering a scratch single to the lead-off batter, the wiry shortstop, who swung wildly at the pitch, getting only a piece of it. The bat slipped from his hands and went spinning into left field, as the ball plopped down between three fielders in short center. The base runner reached first easily, but rounded too far, allowing the right fielder to make a close play of it by rifling a throw to first. Shimazaki's shortstop dove head first back to the bag while the first baseman flagged the ball and then with a sweeping motion that might have added punch to the ball's already fierce momentum applied what looked to be an unnecessarily rough tag to the base runner's left shoulder. The umpire declared the base runner safe, the dust settled and the opposition coach showed his first sign of emotion, coming out on the field a few feet before stepping back into the dugout. Shimazaki came out of his dugout too in order to attend to his player, shaken up on the play but apparently not injured.

"Even with two outs," one announcer said, "it's hard to imagine they'll have a better opportunity than this."

"I'd have to agree," the other announcer said. The little league pitcher walked toward the batter's box. "We'll get to see what these tenth-graders are made of."

Toshio would have liked to find out. With two outs and two strikes against him, the kid risked striking out on even a foul tip and laid a perfect bunt down the first base line. All of a sudden there were two men on base with Hideki's team's best hitter approaching the plate. The all-star paused just outside the batter's box, nodded to his teammates on first and second, then looked to the dugout for instructions. Now the other coach walked out to the mound, deciding that the .512 batting average this athlete brought into the game made an intentional walk the wiser move. The bases were loaded now, two outs. Shimazaki's clean-up batter dusted his hands against his pants in the on-deck circle and stood up to approach the plate, but suddenly Shimazaki was a blaze of action, calling back his hitter, pointing to the corner of the dugout. Toshio was not sure what was happening, but out of the shadow of the dugout he saw Hideki emerge. "Nozomi!" he yelled. "Nozomi! Nozomi! Get off the phone, come here!"

"I'm not on the phone," she said, putting down the afternoon mail. "What is it?"

"Hideki is going into the game!"

The camera pulled back as Hideki took his practice swings. The cheerleaders and song girls were in full force now, the rooting section up. Nine players in the field, three

183

on the bases, Hideki at the plate. The wind played with the national flag back of center. The sky grew darker.

"Shimazaki is a Zen genius," Toshio said.

Hideki took a wild swing, not even close. Strike one.

Shimazaki took a step up from the dugout now, was pumping an imaginary bat as if by proper demonstration in this instant alone he could make up for the years of training and preparation Hideki had never had.

"They don't teach this in *juku*," Toshio said.

The pitcher fired again. High. If Hideki could hold back on his swing, it would be ball one. However at the last moment, Hideki decided he saw something he liked. He took aim and missed. And with the ball out of the strike zone, Hideki looked even wilder this time.

"Why did you do that?" Toshio asked.

"Strike two," the umpire signaled, punching with his right arm.

Shimazaki was up on his feet again, doing cross-windmills this time with both arms in order to catch Hideki's attention. Then with one hand he placed an imaginary ball in front of himself, pointed to it directly with the same hand, put both hands on an imaginary bat and swung through. Hideki nodded and stepped back to the plate.

The next pitch was low and outside. Hideki looked like he was leaning, but either decided it was better not to or else he was too paralyzed to swing. The umpire took a long look at Hideki before announcing his call. "Ball one," he said finally and stepped back from the plate.

Shimazaki applauded from the dugout now with short crisp claps, then ran through his routine again quickly with the imaginary bat and ball. Hiroshi stood by the coach's side, less restrained in his encouragement. The rooting section cheered with military fervor. The pitcher glanced at the plate, looked to his own dugout, checked the man on

184

third base and then allowed himself to look over at the other dugout, at Shimazaki. He delivered. Way high. Almost wild. Hideki did not flinch. "Ball two," the umpire called.

"Good," Toshio said.

The other coach came running out to the mound, concerned that his pitcher had been distracted. Seeing this, Shimazaki employed a new tactic. He allowed Hiroshi to encourage Hideki, while he now focused his energy completely on the opposing pitcher. The other coach did not miss this new development. Walking back to the dugout, he turned his own full attention on Hideki.

He's got the wrong guy, Toshio thought.

The camera focused on Hideki. Toshio looked at his son, thought that Hideki had made up his mind, that regardless of the pitch he was going to swing. He was out of his league in this situation and had no way of directly influencing the events before him. But Toshio knew that like father, like son, it was better not to go down just standing there. Chippy shots were not the way. Hideki was not a trading company. He would swing for the fences. He would go all the way.

Hideki took a few more practice swings, then cocked his bat. The Osaka pitcher entered his wind-up, powerful arms, rocking into a high kick. He delivered. Hideki began his swing. Toshio wondered who looked wilder, the pitcher bearing down like that or Hideki waving his bat. But then as the ball was approaching the plate, it broke down and in. And Hideki checked his swing as the ball continued to break and hit him in the groin. Hideki went down flat. The catcher looked confused. The umpire tried to attend Hideki. Shimazaki bolted out of the dugout, his assistant coach right behind. Hideki's teammates on base stood still. His teammates in the dugout leaped up. The Osaka players in the field walked in toward home, then stopped, then walked in closer again. Even the practiced cheers in the stands abated.

185

The group that surrounded Hideki made it impossible to see what was happening.

"We'll be back after this message," the announcer said.

Advertising, Toshio thought. At a moment like this.

The phone rang. Nozomi looked at her husband. "You take it," he said.

"Yes, Mother," Nozomi said to her mother-in-law, "we saw it. We don't know how he is yet."

The television returned to live action. Hideki struggled to his feet, then limped toward first base. The umpires conferred to the right and back of home plate. Hideki fell once and got up again before reaching first base. Shimazaki would have none of it. He called for Hideki's replacement and had the assistant coach walk Hideki off the field. Shimazaki barked instructions to the assistant coach who disappeared with Hideki into the locker room.

One announcer said that he hoped Hideki was all right. The other said it was one of the more unfortunate things he had seen in recent years in high school sports. The announcers promised to relay more information about Hideki as soon as they received it. Attention returned to the game where the next batter struck out on three pitches. Shimazaki's team returned to the dugout with a 1-0 lead.

In the bottom of the ninth, Osaka team's first batter dueled with Shimazaki's ace by repeatedly fouling off pitches. Finally he found one to his liking and sent a shot deep to center field. The center fielder seemed to lose it momentarily before making the catch. "I would say he lost it in the sun," the announcer said, "but there is no sun."

The second batter took two balls, then fouled out to the catcher. The first pitch to the next batter was a called strike, and then it started to rain. After taking a ball low and outside, the batter hit a slow roller back to the pitcher, who threw him out. The rain turned into a downpour. There was

186

little reaction on the faces of Shimazaki's players except relief. The other team cried.

"I think this is a game people are going to talk about for a long time," one announcer said.

"I would certainly agree," the other announcer responded and then more directly to the television audience, "we'd like to stay on with the post-game show, but due to the extended length of today's game we will return to our regular programming."

There was some shuffling with the mikes. The picture remained of the rain coming down on the field and the vacating stands. "That kid sure got nailed," one announcer said, apparently thinking he was off the air. "Wow."

"I'm sure they went to a doctor," Nozomi said. "Let's keep the phone clear and wait."

The first call was from a reporter. "We don't know," Nozomi said, "we're waiting."

The call from the hospital came not long after. "He's all right," Nozomi said to Toshio. "A bad bruise on the thigh. No damage . . ."

"Let me on the line," Toshio said. "I have to talk with him."

"It's the assistant coach," Nozomi said.

"Moshi, moshi," Toshio said. "This is Hideki's father. I'd like to speak with my son."

There was a pause. Hideki came on. "Dad?"

Toshio took Nozomi's hand. "They didn't get you, did they? I mean . . ."

"They didn't get me, Dad," Hideki said.

Toshio squeezed Nozomi's hand. "It may be a good thing you haven't finished growing yet," he said into the phone.

"Maybe so," Hideki answered.

"Your mother's worried about you," Toshio said, "but we think you did great. We're waiting for you."

"Thanks, Dad," Hideki said.

Nozomi motioned for the phone. "Just a second," Toshio said to Hideki, but by the time he handed Nozomi the phone the line was dead.

The phone rang continuously. Nozomi tried to remain even-tempered as she assured callers that Hideki was all right, but she was sure she sounded impatient at times.

Sanae came home with Natsumi and Natsumi's mother a little later. Sanae had been crying. Nozomi comforted Sanae, but seeing her cry like that brought out her own worst fears. Somehow in the anxiety and the unknowing and then with all the phone calls, Nozomi had not taken time with her own feelings. Toshio was acting a little jumpy too.

Coach Shimazaki called from the phone on the bullet train. It was a terrible connection, but Toshio was pleased to receive the call.

"I'm going to meet the train," he said to Nozomi when they hung up.

It was just as well for Nozomi. In a moment like this she preferred to be alone or alone with Sanae. The two ate the light dinner she put together. Sanae said that she wanted to wait up for Hideki, but when she began to fall asleep, Nozomi escorted her upstairs. It was already past nine. Once or twice Nozomi thought about turning on the videotape machine, but each time she turned it off again quickly. Why watch again?

There were more phone calls. Toshio's mother again. Nozomi had to admit she was being a lot more gracious than she would have expected and was actually able to convey a feeling Nozomi appreciated. Nozomi hesitated before hanging up. And there was another phone call. From a woman who identified herself as the mother of Hideki's friend, the girl who helped with the team. The woman was glad to know that Hideki was not seriously hurt and mentioned in passing that she had been to several games. She wondered if Nozomi would like to attend one. Nozomi had not really thought about it. It was a nice call to receive.

Hideki and the assistant coach arrived home about ten-thirty. Toshio was not with them. "Didn't you see your father?" she asked.

"No," Hideki answered. He looked at the assistant coach.

The assistant coach started to speak, but Nozomi wasn't interested in anything he had to say. "Thank you for bringing Hideki home," she said.

"Are you hungry?" she asked when the assistant coach left. Toshio could find his own way home. He always did.

"Tired," Hideki said and started upstairs.

"Let's see it," Nozomi said.

"The doctor said there's nothing you can do for a bruise."

"I want to see it."

"Come on, Mom. It's nothing." He went into his room.

"I'm your mother," she said. "I want to see it."

Reluctantly he took off his pants and lay down on the bed.

The bruise burned red and purple. "You were lucky," she said and sat down on the bed.

"The doctor said there's nothing you can do for a bruise."

She looked at Hideki's body and thought about the differences between his and Toshio's. Don't, she thought. But it was hard not to. Even the little things—even just seeing Hideki like this—triggered so many feelings. Her loneliness. Feelings about having a husband who was never at home. The tension Toshio's absence created between herself and Hideki. The pressure it put on her own life.

Men, she knew, have relationships with other men's daughters. Women have relationships with their sons.

She thought about Hideki and that girl. What did that girl know about her son?

Hideki touched his mother's hair.

"It hurts, Mom," he said.

"I know."

ELEVEN

Toshio stepped onto the train and thought about Hideki's game. How many times had he replayed that moment in his mind? The way the whole thing seemed to have become almost a national issue. Speculation as to how directly Hideki had really taken the shot. His courage and sacrifice. *Break* had sealed the matter finally with an action sequence that showed Hideki swinging wildly and the ball catching him on the upper-thigh. "Close Call," the caption read, a chilling thought of what might have been. The coaches' association had put out a call for mandatory pre-game inspection to make sure all players were wearing plastic cups in their jocks.

Every conversation in the office now seemed to begin with a five-minute discussion related to Hideki. A run-down of the game, the decision to allow Hideki to leave *juku* and join the team, Coach Shimazaki. Toshio tried to maneuver these conversations so as not to have to explain that he was not at the game. Toshio was never one to turn away from a little interest or attention, but the deluge of calls was almost too much. There was a certain relentlessness to the inquiries, a feeling that beneath the kindness people were only looking for trouble, a hope that Hideki was hurt. "And how is Matsuzaka, Jr.?" Shun Ozaki liked to ask.

The train was crowded. Toshio felt tired. There had been another development as well. His mother had called with the news. The likelihood that his brother Kazuo would be receiving a new title at work. "Didn't he tell you?"

"No," Toshio had said. What does he ever tell me? He thought about his brother. If Kazuo could succeed he should be able to as well.

Toshio felt tense. He surveyed the train but could see little of interest. His thoughts turned to Yuko. Yuko, his model, poster girl, prospective talent. These pictures give me no bust, he imagined she was complaining in his office.

Come here, he thought. When was that meeting?

He took out his pocket calendar. Every morning Toshio made an outline of the things he hoped to accomplish that day, balanced it against the commitments he had already made and turned it all into some kind of schedule. Every morning he made a schedule and every afternoon he threw it out.

Toshio picked up a discarded magazine from the overhead rack and turned through the ads looking for inspiration.

The train ride seemed to be taking longer than usual. What was the delay? Toshio felt uncomfortable. His clothing was uncomfortable. The train seemed hotter and more crowded. Someone shuffled against him. When the train arrived at the station one of the doors jammed and the crowd backed up. Some shoving started behind him. It felt like someone was climbing on his back. There was only so much time. A young man tried to cut in front of him. Toshio threw a short right forearm to clear the way, a little push, and then walked into the station.

Slowly Toshio became aware of a woman and child holding hands and walking alongside. Although Toshio could not see the woman clearly, something about her prompted him to move closer. She seemed to be heading toward one of the department stores. Toshio followed at a safe distance, misdirecting his attention from time to time so as not to be discovered. Toshio did not know why he had developed this habit of following women, but he did know to do so carefully.

"Sir . . ." Tahara was hovering above Toshio's desk almost immediately.

"What is it, Tahara?"

"Just to let you know we're all set for the party. Everything is taken care of."

"Good, Tahara," Toshio said. "Thank you."

"I have some other news that might please you," Tahara said with a grin. "We received a request this morning from the editor of a teen magazine that wants to feature Miss Tanioka on its cover."

Toshio nodded. He had just been thinking about her.

"And we also got a call," Tahara continued, "regarding an appearance for Miss Tanioka on an after-school children's television special. Not the lead, but a good role. I wanted to tell you. I thought they might be good signs."

For what, Toshio thought, the greatest embarrassment of my professional life? He'd had a growing desire to cancel the whole thing in order to avoid the fiasco it seemed likely to become. The feelings had intensified since hearing "Dreamy, Thinking of You." "What's happening with Yuko?" Toshio asked. "Is everything all right with Yuko?"

"She's fine," Tahara said.

"What is it, Tahara?" He could always tell when Tahara was trying to hide something.

Tahara knew it was better not to resist his boss. "She's fine," he said, "except that she's broken out with a pimple."

192

"Where?" Toshio asked.

"On her nose," Tahara said.

"Have you seen it?"

"You can't miss it," Tahara said. "It's the biggest pimple I've ever seen."

"Can't she go to a doctor?" Toshio asked. "What did Aihara say?" Where was Aihara?

"He was a little concerned about it," Tahara said.

"And?"

"Aihara asked Hideo Ota what we should do."

"What did Ota say?"

"Ota said that one pimple is all right. Two and we're in trouble."

Toshio laughed. Maybe he had been too hard on Tahara.

Mitsue buzzed. "We have an American in the reception area," she said. "He says he has an appointment."

"With whom?" Toshio asked. He looked at his book. "Did you make an appointment without telling me, Mitsue?"

"No," she said, "but it's the same man who was here before."

Toshio looked at Tahara. "Krane?"

"Mr. Ted Krane," Mitsue said, "and his interpreter."

Krane was paging through a magazine as Toshio and Tahara approached. "How are you?" he asked as he stood up.

"How are you?" Toshio said. He looked at his guest. Krane was wearing a gray pin-stripe suit. A little flashy perhaps, Toshio thought, by Japanese standards, but the man looked good.

"I'm fine, thank you," Krane said. He handed Toshio an attractively wrapped gift. "I assume you got my fax."

"Doomo," Toshio said, accepting the gift, *"arigato gozaimashita."* The office would have to send something over for Krane, he thought. "Fax? I don't think so. Please,

193

why don't we move into my office? Mitsue," he inquired while passing her desk, "did we receive a fax I don't know about?"

"I don't think so."

"Check it," Toshio said, escorting the group into his office.

"I brought the financial statements," Krane said, handing Toshio a large envelope. "How is everything?" Toshio and Tahara seemed a little uncomfortable with the familiarity of this question. Krane tried to make conversation, but it was difficult.

"Well, I guess I should probably get to the point," Krane said. "I realize it's still premature, but I want to let you know that I do have a green light from home office to talk turkey. We've made a commitment to go with Japan, and I'll tell you something else, I like Diamond Advertising."

Toshio looked at Krane. Maybe it was time, he thought, for the office to start using foreign models in the advertisements.

The translator struggled to understand Krane's expression "to talk turkey." The laboriousness of having to explain this, coupled with the general inappropriateness of Krane's approach, created an awkward moment. When the interpreter finally did understand what Krane was trying to say, her manner betrayed a certain embarrassment at having to relay it.

Toshio looked at the envelope marked "Confidential" that Krane had brought. Maybe that wasn't such a smart idea to have asked for Sweet Wells' financial statements. He had heard stories about how easily American companies got the wrong idea and became excited about prospects. Had he encouraged the same mistake himself?

Mitsue entered with four cups of tea. Krane looked at Toshio. "I know most people assume it's our experience

194

with U.S. media that makes us so attractive to our partners, but I think the way we've been of most service to our affiliates is through our creative department. Creative," Krane said. He knew it was a losing battle. Sweet Wells had no lock on anything proprietary. Wouldn't the media just as well sell to anyone in the end?

"How exactly does this work?" Toshio asked.

Krane tried to explain, but what seemed so logical at the weekly meetings in New York sure didn't sound as good here. "Because it avoids a duplication of efforts," he said finally.

"Tahara," Toshio asked, "can you think of a time it might make sense for us to send work to New York?"

"I would have to think about it," Tahara said.

"Maybe when the right thing comes along we could send it to New York and see how it goes," Toshio said. "By the way, how do you like Japan?"

"How do I like Japan?" Krane replied. "I really like it."

"Don't love Japan too much," Toshio said.

The two men shared a smile. "I'd like to ask you something," Krane said, "honestly. Don't you think that things are going to open up between our two countries in the future? Don't you think that it makes sense to be ready? I mean with all the attention this has been getting doesn't something have to change?"

"Things have already changed," Toshio said, not entirely comfortable with his tone of voice. "We're much more open than we used to be."

Krane did not respond.

"Of course we know that a lot remains to be done," Toshio continued. "This is a highly complex issue, but let's not overlook the positive. Did you know that Japan imports more from the United States than from any other country? Seventy percent of our oranges come from America now,"

Toshio said. "To be realistic . . . market-opening . . . action program . . . further study . . . consider again. . . ."

The meeting was over. Krane could do the postmortem later in his hotel room. Maybe he would tell his superiors that he had decided to recommend against an affiliation. That Sweet Wells should go it alone in Japan, set up its own office. It was worth a try. What were the alternatives? Better put, what was his alternative?

Time seemed to slow down for Krane as he walked through the bull pen and out of the office. If there was resentment among the workers it sure was hard to find. Krane noticed a word processor one of the women was using. A word processor that could accommodate the Japanese language. This office was humming and it was humming without him, without Sweet Wells.

"This is where I'm staying," Krane said and handed Toshio a card from his hotel. "If there's anything you would like to discuss, please give me a call."

Toshio showed his guest to the elevator. If nothing else, Toshio thought, it was a good experience. Nothing bad had happened. He liked Krane. And it was over.

Toshio stepped into the bathroom on his way back to the office. Haircut, he thought while looking in the mirror.

Mitsue was speaking with Hiroto Itoh on the phone as Toshio approached.

"Matsuzaka," Itoh said when Toshio picked up. He sounded like a little boy. "Matsuzaka, what time do the fireworks begin?"

"Six o'clock," Toshio said, "didn't they tell you?"

"That's what I thought," Itoh said. "I'm just checking. I've arranged for a car."

"No kidding," Toshio said.

"No kidding."

196

The afternoon passed quickly. Mitsue found the copy she had made of the fax they now understood had been sent by Ted Krane. Toshio decided to open the present Krane had brought. It was a book about advertising written in English. As he thumbed through the pages Toshio thought back to a meeting held years before to review a product one of the clients wanted to introduce—an extra-strength pine-scented air freshener. "Excuse me," the client had said. To demonstrate the product's effectiveness the client took out another small bottle that when opened gave off what was worse than a putrid smell, and then sprayed the room with the air freshener. "Isn't that something?" he asked. "Tell me what that smells like." Toshio knew what it smelled like— the same in every language. He put the book, Krane's gift, on his bookshelf.

Toshio called Tahara into his office about 3:25 p.m. It might be difficult sometimes to know when the sentence for punishable offenses was up, but Tahara's moment seemed to have just arrived. Toshio looked up from the papers on his desk. "Are we ready?"

"We're ready."

"I assume we'll go over a little early."

Tahara smiled. "I think we should."

Toshio seemed a little uncomfortable.

"What is it?" Tahara asked.

"Do you think," Toshio cleared his throat, "that we have time to get a haircut before the party begins?"

Tahara looked at his watch. "Sure," he said. "Where will you go? The usual?"

The usual place, Toshio thought, where the barber talks too much and his fingers smell like cigarettes? "What about the place where you go?" he asked. "Is it far?"

"No," Tahara said, "it's not far. It's close."

"Good," Toshio said. "See if you can make an appointment."

"I don't think they take appointments."

"Do you think it would be a long wait?"

"I'll see. I have their number at my desk." Tahara walked out to the bull pen.

Toshio picked up the phone. He thought about calling Nozomi but dialed his broker instead. "Matsuzaka," he said into the phone, "how did we close?"

"Up a tick," his broker said, checking. "No, I'm wrong. Down a tick."

"Participation?" Toshio demanded.

"Mostly commercial," his broker answered.

"Any news?"

"Talk about the American deficits."

"Anything else?" There was talk about the American deficits whether the market went up or down.

"Nothing," his broker answered. "We're dead around here."

"Thank you," Toshio hung up.

"They'll take us, Chief," Tahara said from the door.

"Oh," Toshio said, "good. How do we get there?"

"We can walk," Tahara said. "It's close."

"We'll take a taxi." Toshio took one more look at his appointment book. "I'm going out," he told Mitsue, walking past her desk. "Probably be out until the party." He eyed his "in box" as if she might have forgotten something.

"All clear," she said.

The taxi had a small television set mounted inside on its ceiling that played video-recorded advertisements. "Excuse me," Toshio said to the taxi driver, "is it necessary to have this on right now?"

198

The driver turned it off. The taxi was also equipped with a *karaoke* singing sound system.

"We're here," Tahara said.

"Where?" The meter hadn't changed.

The shop was different. To begin with, women were having their hair cut as well. The wait was longer than it needed to be, and Toshio felt he wasn't getting the full attention he deserved. Toshio did not recognize several of the magazines lying on the tables and when it was time for his shampoo the girl did not massage hard enough. Everyone smelled funny, like they were from a different generation—sickly sweet with a metallic touch of adolescent hormone. They are from a different generation, he thought.

"What can I do for you?" Toshio's "cutter" asked when a chair finally opened. "My name is Shinji." Shinji handed Toshio what looked like a menu. Instead of food there were pictures of different hair styles. Half of the models wore sunglasses. Toshio looked at Tahara who was overseeing the operation from a corner of the waiting area. Tahara nodded. "What would you like?" Shinji asked.

"The same, only shorter," Toshio said.

"I can't give you a cut," Shinji said.

"Why not?"

"Because with that head of hair you need a style."

I have straight black hair, Toshio thought, why do I need a style? Tahara came over from the waiting area. Shinji was adamant. What could happen? Toshio asked himself. It was too late to make other arrangements. One of the pictures on the menu actually had some appeal. "What about this one?"

"I like it on you," Shinji said. Tahara went back to the waiting area and lit a cigarette. Shinji started talking. Toshio fell asleep.

After a few minutes, Tahara came over. Toshio awoke while Shinji was finishing with the blow-dryer. Toshio looked at himself from all angles with a hand-held mirror. "Can we change everything?" he asked.

"You'll like it when you get used to it," Shinji said. "I bet you'll even like it tomorrow morning."

When I wake up, Toshio thought, and it's all pushed over to one side or scrunched up into a cone. "What do you think, Tahara?"

"It goes without saying."

"What," Toshio asked, "goes without saying?"

"It goes without saying," Tahara repeated.

"Well, if it goes without saying," Toshio said, "then it goes with saying, too. Say it." Toshio decided to repress further judgement in order to avoid strangling Tahara on the spot. Other options seemed limited. He looked at his watch and stood up. "How much does this cost?"

"I took care of it," Tahara said. "Don't worry."

"I'm not worried," Toshio said. They walked out to the street. "I guess not everyone who goes to the beauty parlor will come out beautiful. Am I right, Tahara?"

"I don't know," Tahara said. "I like it."

"That's very funny," Toshio said and put his hand on Tahara's shoulder, "but you don't have to pretend with me, okay?"

"I really like it," Tahara said. "I think it makes you look younger."

"You think what?"

"I think that it makes you look younger," Tahara said.

Oh?

They headed for the subway. Nobody at the party will say anything, Toshio thought, but everyone is going to be looking.

Seeing the men—the Diamond Advertising men—waiting in the rented hotel reception area, Toshio could understand how much pressure each was under, the need to maintain a feeling of harmony and the need to avoid a mistake. "Yes." "Isn't that so?" "Really?" "Is that right?" Responses that didn't necessarily indicate agreement, but meant that someone was there, that someone was listening. It was another way of covering the space, of covering almost every inch in a small country where nothing went uncounted. It was easy to understand the convenience of having the verb at the end of the sentence: one could change, soften or modify the entire meaning depending on the reaction one was getting.

Toshio looked at the bar. He had heard it said many times that when drunk a man could throw out the rules and say whatever he wanted. Toshio had heard it, but the truth was he knew his men too well to buy it completely. Being drunk was just another set of circumstances. A little more latitude perhaps as to subject matter, a little more allowance for sentimentality. It was easier when drinking, more fun when drunk. But whoever thought alcohol meant a total release just did not understand how deeply they were all held in the common web. Even when drinking that pressure was there.

Toshio looked at his men. Aihara was present. Yamamoto too. Tahara, of course. Shibata was forcing fluids, a technique he had heard boosted stamina. "Where's Saeki?" Toshio asked. Saeki should be doing this too.

No one seemed to know. Toshio continued his inspection of the room. Everything seemed to be all right, but now the men were following him. "Tahara," Toshio said, "we need more ashtrays in here." He felt he had to say something. Was it a rule that one's best clothing also had to be the most uncomfortable?

The first guest arrived. Tatsu Taguchi—the Flamingo Restaurant chain. Toshio had been with Diamond Advertising for almost twenty years. The firm has a party to honor its clients, and the first guest to arrive has been an account for three weeks.

Taguchi talked about the horse races. He said that he had been to the track the other day and just missed a nice hit. Taguchi picked cashews out of the mixed nuts while speaking. His conversation indicated he was still in elementary school as far as gambling was concerned. Toshio was glad to see Hiroto Itoh walk in the door.

"Matsuzaka," Itoh called in a deep, hoarse voice. The entire room turned to face him. That man could really throw his voice into second gear. He walked over to Toshio. "Where's Saeki?" he asked, looking over Toshio's shoulder.

Hideo Ota arrived next. He winked at Toshio as he entered. The rest of the guests arrived soon afterwards. There must have been almost thirty men there besides Diamond Advertising's own salarymen.

The party had not really taken off, but everything was going pretty smoothly with one exception: an almost unbelievable error on the part of Takashi Muraoka of Maruichi Bank, whom Toshio now wished he had not invited. The party was for Diamond Advertising clients, not prospective clients or friends. Muraoka's error was to invite a young man, who Toshio learned on exchange of business cards, was from Denko Incorporated, one of the nation's largest and most competitive advertising agencies. Toshio had heard of some pretty low things in his career. The situation made him furious. "Denko?" he asked.

"Sumimasen," his competitor said, "I'm pleased to meet you."

Sumimasen, Toshio thought, eyeing his competition. Did the boy really know the meaning of this word, comprehend the reference to obligation and responsibility that comes with being part of a group? That he too belonged to a society that does not threaten its other members by crowding onto unwelcome turf. *Sumimasen*—an obligation and responsibility that never ends.

Toshio mustered the sum total of his business power, concentrated it into a single hate-filled glance, a look he hoped would poison, and focused singularly on this man from Denko. "Welcome to our party," Toshio said and walked away.

Out of the room. Into the bathroom. Toshio knew himself well enough to clear out for a moment before doing or saying anything rash. Every feeling he had ever experienced about the inequities involved in competing against larger firms, companies whose solvency was virtually guaranteed by the government, now surfaced. Toshio could not think clearly. There was only one thing to do. He would take Ken Kondo aside and explain, ask Ken to sit right on this guy's tail, tie him up and keep him from getting any bright ideas.

Toshio washed his hands and face before realizing there were no paper towels to dry with, only a blow dryer on the wall. "Improves sanitation," it read. Saves money, he thought. There was water all over the place. He looked at himself in the mirror and took out his comb. What a haircut, he thought, but it was too late now. The party, he remembered suddenly, what are you doing in here looking at yourself in the mirror? It's either him or me, Toshio concluded about the man from Denko, and in this case it's going to be me.

Shun Ozaki was stepping out of the room as Toshio approached. "Where is it?" he asked.

"Back and to the left," Toshio said.

"Nice party," Ozaki said. He headed for the bathroom.

Why go to Ken Kondo for help? Toshio thought. Ozaki knew what to do in situations like this. Ozaki was already up the mini-flight of stairs. Toshio felt a keen sense of embarrassment as he approached Ozaki, but he had to do it.

"What is it, Matsuzaka?" Ozaki asked.

"I have to ask you," Toshio said, "did you know that there's a man from Denko at our party?"

"I spoke with him," Ozaki said. "He gave me his card." Ozaki reached into his coat pocket and shuffled through twelve or fifteen business cards before finding the man's. "Here," he said.

"Doesn't it seem strange to you this guy would attend our party?" Toshio asked.

"He seems like an all right guy to me," Ozaki said. "I don't think I would worry about it."

Even if he is an all right guy, Toshio thought, you talk to one member of a family and you're talking to all of them. "I don't think he should be here," Toshio said. "I know about competitors trying to steal clients, competitors trying to steal ideas."

"Do you?" Ozaki asked.

"Don't you?" Toshio replied.

Ozaki thought before speaking. "I wish my competitors would steal your ideas," he said and chuckled. He turned and walked toward the bathroom.

Back in the party Toshio headed for the bar until he noticed that everyone seemed to have been waiting for him. "Like the magnificent bamboo," Itoh raised his glass and began what would develop into a series of toasts and speeches, allowing his discourse to touch on any number of subjects before ending with a confession that he had originally approached Diamond Advertising after looking through a phone book.

"Well, that's advertising too," someone said.

Yamamoto toasted Toshio on behalf of the salarymen. "I know I speak for everyone here when I say that if there was ever a time or a place . . ."

Toshio was afraid that Yamamoto had lost his way.

"Truly," Yamamoto said, "if there was ever anything we could do for you, if you ever needed a favor or . . ."

Don't do me any favors, Toshio thought.

When Yamamoto was done, Toshio responded with a little speech of his own, individually recognizing and acknowledging the role that each of his clients had played in Diamond Advertising's development. After Toshio finished and the men had drunk, Shibata waved the group together for a picture. Toshio hoped that Shibata had remembered the film.

The clients and salarymen moved together for the group shot. Toshio couldn't help but notice how stiff Muraoka looked in front of the camera. Diamond Advertising had done some work for a small bank once, a full-page general image advertisement that featured some supposedly candid shots taken of the bank's men to personalize the bank's image. Toshio remembered what a headache it had been to get the bankers to look natural before the camera, how difficult it had been to get them to relax.

Shibata handed the camera to the man from Denko who acted like a pretty good sport about the whole thing. Toshio tried not to let the situation affect his smile, but it wasn't easy. As the group was breaking its pose, Toshio heard a click from behind. Hideo Ota had photographed the group from the rear.

The party broke up at nine; Diamond Advertising had reserved the room for just that long. About half the guests said good-bye and left. The other half stood just outside the room talking, as if anticipating something further. Toshio assumed they would go on to drink somewhere else. He hoped that Muraoka and the man from Denko would disappear. Unfortunately these two seemed to have a different idea. Muraoka especially was hanging around Toshio, seemed to have taken a special liking to him and was always trying to talk to him or touch him on the arm when he couldn't get his attention otherwise.

The party began to move out. Toshio was not sure exactly where they were headed, but the salarymen seemed to have everything under control. Toshio saw Hiroto Itoh and said, "You're still here."

"Get in," Itoh said, pointing to the car he had hired. It was down to the core now, the fifteen or eighteen men around whom Toshio's livelihood depended. He was not surprised that Aihara and Ota had disappeared.

The men split up into taxis, at least one salaryman in each group. Muraoka wanted to join Toshio in Itoh's car, but the car had already filled. Toshio was glad. He could see the salarymen were watching Muraoka and the man from Denko more carefully now. The office organism was working to protect itself. Ken Kondo seemed able to relax a little more. Toshio felt better too. Sit down, he told himself.

The first destination was Applause. The *mama-san* stood by the door to greet the men as they entered. She was not a woman who had aged well, and Diamond Advertising had been going there for a long time.

"Mama, come here," Toshio said when he sat down. She started pouring whiskey and water, but she seemed to be pouring stronger tonight.

"A man and wife have three children," Taguchi said. "All three are girls and the wife is pregnant again. What odds do you want that her next baby is a girl?"

The men argued back and forth on this for awhile until Shun Ozaki said that he would walk away from the situation. "A house with three girls?" he asked. Everybody laughed and agreed with Ozaki.

The conversation turned next toward Ken Kondo. It always did. Kondo who traveled through Korea, the Philippines, Thailand and Taiwan leading tours of Japanese

206

businessmen to get laid. Maybe it was better to do this away from home, Toshio thought, but then he knew another thing as well. That to really understand Japan it was important to see the other Asian countries as well. To really understand how the Japanese acted among themselves and with guests at home it was necessary to see how they behaved and had behaved overseas.

"The difference," Kondo said, "between developed countries and developing countries is one, insects fly faster in developing countries. Don't ask me why, but they do." The men were listening. "And two," Kondo said, looking around the room and lowering his voice for effect, "generally speaking, women don't like to give head in developing countries."

"What about the men?" someone asked.

"Men don't like to give head anywhere."

"What about a blow job given with an ice cube in the girl's mouth?" one of men asked. "Have you heard of that?"

"It's called a blow job on the rocks," Kondo said. "I'm serious."

The *mama-san* turned on the snack's *karaoke* system. Toshio stood up and moved to the front of the room to supervise the passing of the mike. After singing the usual Japanese standards—"North Country Spring," "The Boatman's Song," "Mother"—the party turned to the tunes Toshio liked best: "Diana," "Michelle," "I Left My Heart in San Francisco."

Toshio soloed on "My Way." When he finished Muraoka stood up and insisted that Toshio lead a group rendition of the same. Toshio's protests would not be heard. The music picked up. About a third of the men were on their feet now, belting lyrics of this salaryman's anthem at each other. When the song was over everyone cheered. Toshio placed the microphone down. The men put on their jackets, rallying toward what Toshio assumed would be the next pit stop.

"We don't know how to spend our time, our money or our vacations," someone said as the group shuffled out, "but we're happy."

In the deepening inebriation Toshio could recall only a montage of impressions as the men moved from one place to another. They must have hit four or five different spots, he thought. He was sure they had not gone to Esprit. He was pretty sure they had not gone to On The Rocks. He did seem, however, to remember all the taxis pulling up in front of a pink salon. "What are we doing here?" he asked.

The hustlers from the various places on the street had gathered and were opening taxi doors and directing the men up.

Tahara had Toshio's arm now. "We rented the place," he said. "We've got it all to ourselves."

"Whose idea?" Toshio wanted to know, but he was distracted by the posters of young girl singers plastered on the walls.

At the top of the stairs Toshio was greeted by one of the hosts, a man who seemed to know that at least for tonight Toshio was the central pillar. "If there are any problems," he said, "just let me know."

"There won't be any problems," Toshio said, noticing that the girls were all dressed in white nurses uniforms. Maybe it wasn't such an inappropriate idea after all, he thought.

The booths had been opened up somewhat and arranged so that the group could be together more easily. The girls poured beer and served little trays of hors d'oeuvres, acting more like hostesses in a snack. There was none of the time pressure Toshio had felt before. He didn't feel like the girls were in it just for the money. It must have cost a fortune, he thought.

208

"I'm sorry that we didn't have more time to talk," the man from Denko imposed himself on Toshio, "I had heard so much about you. I was glad we could at least meet."

"That's fine," Toshio said and turned away. Unfortunately Muraoka seemed to be staying.

There was another round of toasts. "To my friend, Toshio Matsuzaka," Ken Kondo lifted his glass, but paused before speaking, "what words cannot express."

Toshio watched the men drink. He could see several of his salarymen slowing down, losing their energy. But not Kondo, the man was a monster with the sauce. Toshio stood up. "To my friend Ken Kondo," he said, "I announce a founding contribution on the part of Diamond Advertising to the Ken Kondo Home for Foster Children."

"And what kind of contribution is that?" Kondo replied.

Toshio noticed Tatsu Taguchi and Takashi Muraoka pair off with two of the "nurses." Toshio had not been to this place before. The girls were attractive. He had inhibitions with his clients and salarymen present, but these inhibitions were not insurmountable.

The host pushed Toshio toward a girl who seemed to be waiting for him in the corner. She smiled. Toshio noticed Tatsu Taguchi taking a hand job in the booth next door. He turned his attention instead to the other side of the room where Kondo was already talking with two girls. That Kondo, Toshio thought. He headed over.

"Looks to me like there's a lot of talent in this place," Kondo said.

The girls looked so young. Toshio liked young girls. He had a bad case of what was often called "Lolicon." Lolita complex.

"You know our guest of honor is getting into production," Kondo said to the girls who giggled. He gave Toshio the little nod.

Something about the way these girls stood suggested that they had achieved developed nation status themselves. Why not? Toshio asked himself.

"Take him over there," Kondo indicated to the girl who seemed the younger of the two. She looked to be about sixteen. She took Toshio's beer and led him to a booth. Toshio felt like they were farther apart from the other men now, but he could still see Kondo.

The girl touched Toshio on his arm, his knee. She ran her hand up and down his thigh. He leaned back as she moved higher. Let his head fall back as she took him out of his pants. He closed his eyes. It felt good. Real good. She knew what she was doing.

"Why are you stopping?" he asked. There was a rustling by the doorway he did not understand.

"Police," he heard. Police? What was the problem? They had rented out the place. He looked at his watch. It wasn't that late.

Toshio tucked himself in and moved to get up. Just what the company needed on a night like this, he thought, trouble.

One of the policeman retracted the identification he had shown. "We understand there are underaged girls working in this establishment."

Some of the clients started for the door. "Hold it right there," the policeman said.

As the officer turned his flashlight on Tatsu Taguchi, Toshio began to realize the possible implications of this moment. He, his most important clients, and his staff all implicated by the police in an affair involving underaged girls. The officers were standing everybody up and holding two of the girls in particular. One of the girls looked too young, like she was twelve.

"Excuse me, Officer," Toshio said.

There was too much noise, too much confusion. "Hey!" Ken Kondo yelled. "Let's have some quiet in here!"

"Excuse me, Officer," Toshio said, stepping forward, but trying to remain as calm as possible, "do you think there's a way this might be handled more discretely?"

"We've had it with warnings," the policeman said. "You just don't listen."

"Well," Toshio said, "I know that some people don't listen, but I think this group would listen. Why make a major affair out of an inadvertent mistake?"

The officer seemed to soften. He turned to check with the other policemen.

"He's right," Hiroto Itoh said and stepped forward. He took a huge wad of cash out of his pocket.

No, Toshio thought. Not like that.

The officer bristled. "I'm not going to be insulted."

"He wasn't trying to insult you," Toshio said. The policeman wouldn't listen.

"Please, Officer," Itoh said, "couldn't you give us another chance?"

"You'll get your chance," the officer said. "Come here."

"What are you talking about?" Shun Ozaki demanded from the other side of the room. "We weren't doing anything. Leave him alone." He started for the door.

What is Ozaki doing? Toshio thought.

"That's enough out of you," the policeman said. He walked over to slap a pair of handcuffs on Shun Ozaki, and then he walked back and put Hiroto Itoh on the other end.

"Officer," Shibata cried, "please take me instead!"

"What did you do?" the policeman asked. "I want these two."

"You can't do that to us," Ozaki said. He turned toward Toshio with an expression that read, "I am going to kill you." "This is your party, Matsuzaka," he said. "Can't you do something about this? Are you just going to stand there?" Toshio looked at Shun Ozaki; he looked at Hiroto Itoh. Itoh looked sick.

A flashbulb went off. "Press," Toshio heard.

"Press," the policeman said, "that's fine with me. I'd be happy to make an example out of this group."

Toshio grabbed the camera. "Don't anybody move!" he yelled. He wrestled with the camera, hoping to expose the film. The camera wouldn't open.

Itoh started laughing. Toshio couldn't see why. Just because he couldn't get the camera open, there was still nothing funny about the situation. Itoh was standing next to a policeman and handcuffed to Shun Ozaki. What was funny about that? Ozaki started laughing now too. Kondo. Why?

"Happy Birthday!" someone yelled. One of the girls came out from the back with a cake. "Happy Birthday, Diamond Advertising," it read.

Toshio looked at the group and almost passed out. For a second he did not know who they were or why they were there. "Come here," he said finally to the twelve year-old who was standing against the wall. "Come here and blow out these candles." The men applauded. Aihara and Ota appeared in the doorway. Toshio felt like giving the twelve year-old a big kiss, but decided not to. With the lights on, the policemen's uniforms did not even look that real. So what if they had gotten the date wrong? Toshio didn't care. He looked at Aihara and Ota by the door.

"Whose idea?" Toshio asked. "Saeki too? You guys are the worst bunch of actors I've ever seen. You had me fooled so badly. . . . Whose idea?"

Nobody would take credit, but the backward glances all seemed to point toward Tahara. Tahara, then Aihara.

The men started to drink again.

"Some of you may know," Toshio said, after things had settled down and tapping his glass to get the group's attention, "that Diamond Advertising has been thinking about setting up an office overseas."

There was some confusion about this, a murmuring, a little applause. Rumors had been flying in the office with Ted Krane's second visit.

"America?" someone asked.

"No," Toshio said, "not America. I've decided that we're sending Tahara to open an office in North Korea."

The men laughed and drank some more. More toasts, more drinking. The men drank to the Japanese woman— "Who knows where we itch," Shun Ozaki said.

They drank to friendship, to good fortune, to friends who took the trouble. And they drank, as Toshio put it, "To this glittering moment we call life."

TWELVE

The salarymen took the stairs up, unlocked the door and went directly to the closet in the computer room that held the sleeping mats. Toshio groggily thought about Shibata urinating on the stairwell and then . . . he fell asleep . . .

Yuko arrived on time. Toshio looked at his model, singer, poster girl, star. "How are you, Yuko?" he asked. The girl looked terrific. She was cute, young, and gave every appearance of being not only enthusiastic but trouble-free. What was all this business about a pimple?

"I'm fine, thank you," she said. "How are you?"

Toshio nodded. "Make a note, Tahara," he said. "I think we'll want to arrange bodyguard service for Miss Tanioka." He winked.

Tahara smiled. "Excuse me, sir," he said, "there are a few things I should take care of at my desk."

"Of course," Toshio said, "that's fine."

Tahara left the room.

"How are you, Yuko?" Toshio asked again.

"I'm fine," she said. "Maybe a little nervous."

214

"That's natural," Toshio said. "We may be close to some very exciting things here." She was wearing those white boots again. "How are our dancing lessons going?"

"Fine," she said, "although mostly I've been concentrating on singing. I'm trying to learn all the new songs."

We'll put the words on a prompter so you don't forget, he thought. He looked at her boots, her stockings. When you play you can never forget about work, but when you work you can never forget about play. There was a knock on the door. "Yes?" Toshio asked.

Mitsue opened and entered with a middle-aged woman. "I'm sorry I'm late," the lady said to Yuko. "Fumiko Tanioka," she turned to Toshio, "Yuko's mother." Mrs. Tanioka was not an attractive woman. Tall and gangly. A painful smile.

"Won't you have a seat?" Toshio asked. Seeing mother and daughter together like this was not encouraging.

"I'm sorry my husband could not be here," she said, placing herself squarely in the seat of the chair. "We felt that with Yuko's career developing like this I should take an apartment in the city. I guess we have you to thank for all of this."

Toshio now knew that this woman would accompany her daughter every step of the way, would watch over every aspect, every detail of her blossoming career.

"Yuko tells me there's the possibility of an afternoon television special," she said. "Have you seen the script?"

"I'm sorry, sir," Tahara interrupted from the door.

"What is it, Tahara?" Toshio asked.

"Ted Krane is on the phone, sir."

"What does he want?"

"I don't know. Line three."

Toshio hesitated.

"Line three," Tahara repeated.

Toshio picked up.

"How's it going?" Krane's interpreter asked.

How's it going? Toshio thought, that's a pretty personal question. Krane must have insisted on a word-for-word translation. "I'm fine," Toshio said. "Please wish our guest a safe trip back to the United States."

"Thank you very much for the gift," the interpreter said.

"It was nothing," Toshio said, "believe me."

"If it's not too much trouble . . ." the interpreter began.

"Just a second," Toshio said. "Tahara, take the rest of this call at your desk in the bull pen, please."

"Yes sir."

"That reminds me," Mrs. Tanioka said. "I want to give you our home telephone number. I guess we'll be a team from now on."

Unfortunately, Toshio thought.

"I'm going to give you our home phone number," she said, "in case you need to be in contact for any reason."

Toshio looked at Mrs. Tanioka. She was wearing so much make-up. For that matter, Yuko was too. Pancake look, he thought. Or in the case of Yuko's mother, *okonomiyaki*-look. Pizza-pancake. "Excuse me," Toshio said, "would either of you like a cup of coffee?"

"Thank you," Mrs. Tanioka said.

"Yuko?" Toshio asked.

"If it's not too much trouble."

"No trouble. I'll be right back." Toshio stepped out of his office. "Mitsue," he said, "three cups of coffee, please." He looked at Saeki's desk. Even for Saeki it looked too neat. "Where's Saeki?"

"He's not here," Mitsue answered.

"Did you try him at home?"

"No."

"Why not?"

Shibata, Yamamoto and two other salarymen now quickly joined Toshio in the conference room. The group looked a lot thinner without Saeki. "He's going to work for a trading company," Yamamoto said.

"No established company hires a salaryman at this point in Saeki's career," Toshio said. "He's not going anywhere." It said enough about an employee that he would even think about finding another position. Saeki would be lost without Diamond Advertising. "Which trading company?"

"A small trading company," Yamamoto said.

Oh, for the days gone by, Toshio thought, when people willingly sacrificed their own needs and desires for the strength of the group. Saeki? Why would Saeki throw it all away? "Times have not changed that much," Toshio said. "Why would he do this?"

"He has a cousin in the United States," Shibata said. "They found a sponsor and they want to do some exporting."

Good luck, Toshio thought. Now everybody and his cousin were selling to the United States. Was it that easy?

Miho knocked and entered with a package for Toshio's review. The return address showed that the package was from Denko. "For you," she said.

"Thank you," Toshio said. You're pretty, he thought.

"I don't think Saeki intends to compete," Yamamoto continued.

Harmony, Toshio thought about the situation with Saeki—not personal likes and dislikes. He considered the steps he should take. In the short term there would be no problem. Each of the salarymen had at some point been involved with every aspect of the company's operation; in circumstances such as these any member of the group could fill in or one person could do the work of two. In the longer term, however . . .

217

Each of the men spoke in self-effacing terms about how he might have played a part in Saeki's departure and about what could be done to prevent such an event from recurring in the future. The consensus was that the firm should devote more time to discussion related to the underlying factors.

But not too much more time, Toshio thought.

The men walked out. Toshio picked up the package from Denko. What could Denko want? He opened it. "Proposal for The Aoki Chemical Corporation," it read, "Building Better Lives. Submission by Denko Incorporated in association With the Diamond Advertising Company." Inside was a run-down of the theme, a proposed media schedule, responsibilities and fees—142 pages long; 142 pages of formality. Toshio knew what it meant. It meant that they were it. Diamond-Denko, he thought. Or Denko-Diamond. What difference did it make?

Toshio focused on the fees. Denko had set things up to its own advantage, but what did it matter? With the prestige this new collaboration would provide . . . Toshio would really have to do something special for Hiroto Itoh.

Shibata walked back into the conference room. "*Sumimasen,*" he said. "We have the proofs back of the pictures from the party. We're trying to make our selections as quickly as possible to put something together for the clients. A memento."

"I have to see these," Toshio said. The pictures had come out well including, he had to admit, one taken on a separate roll of the policeman and himself before he knew what was happening in the pink salon. The group picture was an obvious choice. Otherwise the overriding factor seemed to be to include at least one shot of each client. Toshio focused on three pictures taken of himself with the man from Denko. Not a good expression—he thought about his scowl—with which to begin an association. "Why don't we take these

218

out?" he suggested, lifting his black felt marker and putting a large "X" through each of the incriminating pictures. "Otherwise I leave it up to you. I don't mind." He indicated that the picture from the pink salon could be included. But it was better to take out the pictures in which he was glaring at the man from Denko. When you do something stupid, he thought, why advertise it?

"Thank you," Shibata said.

"Thank you," Toshio said. He walked back into his office where Yuko and Mrs. Tanioka were waiting. "More coffee?"

"I want to give you our home telephone number," Mrs. Tanioka said.

Why? Toshio wondered. He turned toward Yuko. Why had she taken off her stockings?

"Excuse me, sir," Tahara interrupted from the door.

"What is it, Tahara?" Toshio asked.

"He wants us to write him a letter summarizing the meeting and outlining what steps are necessary to keep alive any possibility of a joint venture."

"Who?" Toshio asked.

"Ted Krane," Tahara said, "the phone call."

"Oh," Toshio said, "what did you say?"

"I said I would discuss it with you."

"Good," Toshio said. "We've discussed it. Now look at this." He handed Tahara the proposal for Aoki Chemical. While Tahara was studying the proposal Toshio walked over to Yuko. "We rented the concert hall," he told her. "We're going to send out the postcards."

Yuko put her hand on his arm. Her touch was so strong, he thought, almost demanding . . .

"Excuse me, sir."

For what? Toshio wondered . . .

He opened his eyes. Tahara? Toshio looked around. His golf clubs were in the corner. No one else was there. A dream, he thought and took a deep breath. A dream, what a morning. . . . "Water, Tahara." He felt like his face had taken on a new fiberglass coating. What was that taste in his mouth? He struggled to his feet.

"Let me help you, sir," Tahara said.

Toshio wrapped a light blanket around his waist and shuffled to the door. He peeked out. Everything seemed fine. He sat down on the sofa. Having been through this before did not make the feeling any better. He closed his eyes. What a dream, he thought, even Ted Krane was preferable to that Mrs. Tanioka. "I'm going home, Tahara. I want to go home and go to sleep."

Tahara held the hanger when Toshio felt ready to don the extra change of clothing he kept for such occasions—the pants, he was aware, did feel a little tighter this time. He looked around the room. "Do we need this?" he asked, pointing to the ice cream maker parked against the wall.

"I don't think so," Tahara said.

"Good. I'm going out," he told Mitsue, as he walked past her desk. "Be out for the rest of the day."

Tahara accompanied Toshio down the elevator. On the street he flagged a taxi.

"*Sayonara*, Tahara." Toshio slid into the back seat.

When the taxi pulled up in front of the house Toshio realized he had left his wallet at the office, in his other pair of pants. "Nozomi," he yelled from the door, "I need some money for the taxi." It's a good thing she was home, he thought.

Nozomi got the money.

In the house he handed her the ice cream maker. "What's this?" she asked.

220

"It's an ice cream maker."

"You didn't need it in the office?" She looked at her husband. "What did you do with your hair?"

"I had it styled," he said. "What do you think?"

I married an idiot, she thought.

He started upstairs.

"Don't you have anything to say?" she asked.

"I'm tired," he said, "exhausted."

"Is that all?"

"The party was fine. I didn't expect to be out so late."

"This is what you have to tell me?"

"We'll have the pictures back in a few days," he said. "I'll show you everything."

"Toshio."

"I'd rather not now, Nozomi." He started up the stairs. "I'm exhausted."

This was the reality, she thought. That it was more acceptable to do some things than to discuss them, considered worse to talk about certain things than to do them.

Toshio could feel her eyes on his back. "Please, Nozomi," he looked down from the top of the stairs, "not now." He turned into the bedroom.

Nozomi walked into the kitchen and picked up the phone. "Akiko," she said, "I thought I might go back to the country this afternoon. Would you mind watching Sanae for me?"

"Of course not," Akiko said. "I'd be happy to. Is everything all right?"

"I didn't have a chance to tell her this morning," Nozomi said, "so I'll leave her a note."

"Understood," Akiko said. "If you're going to be longer you can call me."

Nozomi thought about the last time Akiko, Yukari, Sanae and herself had been together. They had gone for one of

221

those ice treats—shredded ice topped with sweetened milk, sugar water and *azuki* beans. Akiko had ballooned so quickly. "You know how I am," she had said, "I carry heavy."

"Thank you, Akiko." Nozomi hung up. It was a mistake she would never make, whatever the temptation. Reiko might seem like a more natural ally, but Nozomi would always stand with Akiko. Reiko could think only of herself.

Nozomi went upstairs to take out a bag. Toshio was asleep, but stirred. "You're kidding," he said to himself and rolled over.

Nozomi looked at her husband. Each person carries something in his or her own black box, she thought. Something private. Even in marriage.

The train ride was not long. Across the aisle a family rode together. Although the man wore a suit and tie, Nozomi could see the family was on vacation because of all the baggage they were carrying.

From the window Nozomi observed the garden plots that began almost immediately. From time to time she could see a man or woman working in a rice paddy or vegetable garden.

To be able to make a mistake and go home, she thought. To be able to make a mistake at all.

The ride took little longer than an hour. Along the way Nozomi watched the schools and construction, the bridges and the cars. She saw people walking and riding bicycles. She saw buses and she saw children walking together.

At the station Nozomi walked down to the underpass and then up the sixty-seven steps she had counted as a child and never forgotten. She walked slowly now, thinking of the changes. The changes around her and in her own life. About having a family. It was a lot of years together, she thought, a lot of time invested.

Outside the station she was aware of two or three new buildings. She saw a love hotel now tucked off the little main street, visible above what had previously been the rice store. There was another new building too. Downstairs the sign read, "Real Estate." Upstairs, "Girls Wanted." Looking at the sign Nozomi could imagine. Had that kind of thing always been there? Had she missed it before? She didn't know. Even in my own town, she thought, it makes me angry. This is where we are, she realized, divided. Women could not just blame the men. Every time a man was there, some girl was there with him. She understood the complicity.

Nozomi looked up at the houses scattered in the hills— homes of a selfless people. Honest, diligent, hardworking and scared, a people who were perhaps not ready for their future. Whose language even had no future tense.

Like so many people, she thought, we begin with little more than a feeling. We find ourselves raising children, teaching school, working in libraries. We deliver mail, prepare food. We nurse patients and we care for people who can't care for themselves.

We have families like other families. Dreams like other dreams.

She turned toward the trains and the fishermen, the construction workers and the cars.

Never mistake us. Some people are thinking even what they can't say.

Hugh Gross was born in Los Angeles, California, in 1955. He graduated from Yale University, in 1977, with a degree in philosophy.

His first jobs were in financial planning and commodities brokerage. In 1983, he traveled to Asia, working first as a business consultant in Jakarta, Indonesia, and later as an English teacher in Japan and Taiwan.

After returning to Los Angeles, in 1987, Hugh began to write, direct, and produce stage plays, videos, and screenplays.

Same Bed, Different Dreams, his first book, was selected for the 1990 First Novel Series Award sponsored by Mid-List Press.

Hugh is a member of the Dramatist's Guild and the Japan-American Society. He lives in Los Angeles.